He was standing too [close]

"You don't have a favorable opinion of me, do you?" he asked.

"I don't know you."

"And yet you assumed that after you turned me down, I went out and picked up another woman."

She shrugged. "No reason you shouldn't."

"You're the reason I didn't. I couldn't stop thinking about you."

"I have a child," she reminded him.

"You mentioned that." He took a step toward her. "There's definite chemistry between us."

"I don't believe in chemistry."

"No?" He smiled. "Then why is your pulse racing?"

She swallowed. "Because you're crowding me. I don't like to be crowded."

He stroked her cheek, a caress so sensual her blood heated.

"How about being kissed?" he asked, the low timbre of his voice as seductive as his touch. "Do you like being kissed?"

She couldn't remember how it felt to be kissed.

"I'll let you know," she said and pressed her mouth to his.

MATCH MADE IN HAVEN:
Where gold rush meets gold bands!

Dear Reader,

Welcome back to Haven, Nevada, where Patrick Stafford is living the life most men can only dream of. He's got an executive position in the family business, more money than he can spend in his lifetime and the companionship of a willing woman whenever the mood strikes. Why then is he feeling so discontented?

Brooke Langley never dreamed that she'd wind up pregnant before she even graduated from college. Being a single mom was definitely *not* part of her plan, but with the help of her family, she figured out a way to make it work. Now she's got an amazing seven-year-old son and a growing veterinarian practice, and life is good.

So what happens when Patrick decides to walk away from his desk job to open a dude ranch and the local vet who responds to a Valentine's Day call turns out to be the sexiest woman he's ever met?

Cupid's arrow takes aim, of course!

But Patrick has no interest in complicated relationships, and a kid is a major complication. That's okay with Brooke, because she's too busy with real responsibilities to fall for a man who's only playing at being a cowboy—isn't she?

Maybe neither of them is exactly what the other one wants, but it just might turn out that each is exactly what the other one needs.

I hope you enjoy this new chapter in my Match Made in Haven series! Watch for more stories, coming later this year.

Happy reading!

Brenda Harlen

Chapter One

Watching for the arrival of the veterinarian, Patrick Stafford exhaled a relieved breath when he finally spotted a vehicle coming down the long driveway. He didn't recognize either the mud-splattered pickup that parked beside the barn or the woman who exited the vehicle, and the rancher felt a brief twinge of disappointment that his injured horse would have to wait a while longer to be tended. But as a man who appreciated women, his interest was immediately piqued.

She was tall and slender, wearing a sheepskin-lined leather jacket unzipped over a plaid flannel shirt tucked into slim-fitting jeans with a wide brown belt around her waist and well-worn cowboy boots on her feet. Which only meant she was dressed like most of the other women who lived on the ranches that dotted the countryside of Haven, Nevada, and didn't begin to explain why he found himself so drawn to her.

He continued his perusal anyway: long brown hair that was tied away from her face in a neat braid that fell to the middle of her back. As she drew nearer, he realized that her hair wasn't actually brown but auburn, and that it shone with hints of bronze and copper in the afternoon sun. Her eyes were the color of dark chocolate and fringed by long lashes. Her mouth was unsmiling but temptingly shaped. And as his gaze lingered on her lips for just a moment, Patrick realized it had been a long time since he'd kissed a woman—or even wanted to.

He pushed the wayward thought aside to focus on his visitor. "Can I help you?"

"Actually, I'm here to help you." Now her lips curved into a smile and she proffered a hand. "Dr. Langley."

He shook it automatically, noting the long, slender (and ringless!) fingers, neatly trimmed, unpainted nails and firm grip. "Patrick Stafford," he replied automatically. Then her words registered, and he frowned. "You're not Dr. Langley."

"Well, I don't carry a copy of my diploma with me, but I can show you my driver's license," she offered, shifting the backpack he hadn't noticed was on her shoulder so that he could now see the patch bearing the letter *V* superimposed on the staff of Asclepius—the immediately recognizable symbol of her profession.

Apparently she was *a* vet, but he still felt confident in asserting, "I remember Dr. Langley from his visits to Crooked Creek Ranch when I was a kid, and you're definitely not him."

"That would have been my father," she said. "Dr. *Bruce* Langley. I'm Dr. *Brooke* Langley."

Which made sense, as the other Dr. Langley had been older, with salt-and-pepper hair and a stocky build that promised he was capable of handling the ranch animals that were the foundation of his rural practice.

"Where's Ranger?" she asked.

"I might not have been clear when I called," he said now. "But Ranger is a twelve-hundred-pound stallion and rather ornery right now."

"This isn't my first rodeo," she assured him. "It's also not the first time I've been out here to tend to one of Gus Sterling's animals."

"They aren't his animals anymore," he pointed out. "They're mine."

"Right now, I'm more interested in Ranger's injury than in who's paying the bill, but if you want to wait for my father—who's currently tied up out at Whispering Pines helping to birth a breech foal—that's entirely up to you."

Her response didn't eliminate all his doubts, but he decided that if Gus had trusted her with his horses then Patrick could, too. He slid open the barn door and gestured for her to enter.

The heels of her boots clicked on concrete as she made her way down the center aisle to the stallion's stall, but it was the subtle sway of her hips and sweet curve of her derriere that held Patrick's attention. And though he regretted the circumstances that had required

him to contact the veterinarian office, he wasn't sorry
that Dr. Brooke Langley had answered his call.

Haven wasn't so small that everyone knew everyone
else, but there were usually only two or three degrees
of separation between one person and the next. As he'd
already mentioned to Brooke, he remembered her father
from his visits to Crooked Creek Ranch, but he had no
memory of her. And though she must have attended the
same high school he did—because there was only one
in Haven—he drew a blank there, too.

But Ranger seemed to know her, and Patrick was reassured by the animal's acknowledgment of her presence. The stallion's long nose appeared over the door
of his enclosure as she approached and actually seemed
to nod, as if in greeting.

Brooke lifted a hand to rub the horse's cheek, and
Ranger whinnied softly.

Patrick stood back, both mesmerized by the word-
less interaction and a little terrified for the woman who
boldly opened the gate and stepped inside the stall. He'd
guess that she was about five feet eight inches tall, but
next to the horse, she looked small.

And breakable.

Of course, anyone who'd spent any amount of time
around horses had to respect the powerful strength of an
animal whose muscular legs and flashing hooves could
do serious damage, even inadvertently. But Brooke didn't
hesitate to enter the enclosure, and Ranger didn't shy
away from her presence. And somehow, her quiet confidence only added to her allure.

"How are you doing, Ranger?"

Her tone was quiet, soothing, but the hands stroking the animal were steady and sure. Everything she said and did seemed to reassure the animal that she was in charge. Her quiet murmuring trailed off when she crouched down far enough to examine the wound. After a moment's hesitation, she resumed her monologue and continued her study.

When she rose up again and turned to Patrick, her voice was as hard as her gaze. "He's cut all the way through the coronary band. How did this happen?"

"I don't know," he admitted. "I put the horses out in the paddock this morning but somehow Ranger got out and—"

"Somehow?" she interjected.

"I thought I latched the gate, but when I went back to check on the horses, it was swinging free."

"Is Ranger the only one who got out?"

"No, but he's the only one who got hurt."

"I'm going to need more light," she said, reaching over the door for Ranger's halter and lead rope.

It was a testament to Ranger's training—and reassuring to Patrick—that the animal didn't balk in any way as she secured the halter and led him to the crosstie area, where textured rubber mats provided stable footing for both the animal and the vet, and additional lighting illuminated the area even in the dark of night.

He watched as she opened her pack and began rifling through the contents. "He was favoring his right foreleg when I found him."

"No wonder." She unwrapped a syringe, slid the

point of the needle into the vial and measured out the medication.

"This is a tetanus antitoxin," she told Patrick. "He's also going to need a shot of penicillin to combat any infection. Then I'm going to flush the wound and pack it with ichthammol ointment."

"What can I do?" he asked, feeling responsible and guilty and wanting to help.

"You know how to make coffee?" she asked.

He almost breathed a sigh of relief that she'd assigned him a task he could handle. He nodded. "What do you take in it?"

"Black is fine."

"Coming right up," he promised.

While Patrick was gone, Brooke took her time tending to Ranger's injury. She knew the stallion had to be in pain, but at least he seemed to understand that she was there to help. Though initially agitated and skittish—as any wounded creature would be—he stoically endured her ministrations.

In her experience, most animals tolerated necessary treatment if they were given an opportunity to understand that the hands poking and prodding wanted to heal. Sure, she'd endured occasional kicks and nips—and once even a nasty headbutt from a nanny goat that resulted in a concussion—but the veterinarian-patient relationship was generally one of mutual respect and understanding. And if she was ever in doubt, she sedated the animal in the interest of their mutual safety.

She wasn't worried about Ranger. Though pain could

make any man or beast unpredictable, he was a gentle soul. She suspected he was also confused by the change in his circumstances, as evidenced by the departure of the ranch's former owner and the arrival of Patrick Stafford in his stead, and her heart went out to the animal.

"I can't believe Gus left you behind," she lamented aloud. "But maybe there aren't a lot of places to stable a horse in a retirement community in Arizona. And a horse born and bred in Nevada probably wouldn't like Arizona much, anyway."

She'd heard rumors about the old rancher selling, but it was only when she'd turned into the gravel drive and saw the freshly painted barn bearing the new logo of Silver Star Ranch that she realized they were true. A couple of rough years had resulted in the Sterling Ranch teetering on the edge of bankruptcy and one more would have pushed it over, so she could hardly blame Gus for looking for a way out.

But she did blame him for selling to Patrick Stafford— and she definitely blamed the new owner for the horse's nasty injury. The man obviously knew nothing about ranching and even less about caring for the animals that had apparently been entrusted to him as part of the deal.

A deal that would turn the failing ranch into a tourist attraction.

A dude ranch, for Christ's sake.

As if she needed any more proof that Patrick Stafford was just a bored rich guy playing at being a cowboy and opening his doors to other bored rich guys who wanted to do the same thing.

It was only too bad he didn't appear to have the soft,

pale body of a man who'd spent his life behind a desk and under artificial light. Instead, he was tall with broad shoulders and lean hips, looking very much like the rancher he was pretending to be.

And if the checkered shirt with the polo pony embroidered on the chest pocket and distressed designer-label jeans detracted a little from the authenticity of the cowboy image, he was handsome enough to compensate, with sun-bleached sandy-brown hair, tanned skin, surprisingly green eyes, a straight nose, thin lips and a strong jaw shadowed with stubble. But aside from his hard body and striking good looks, he possessed an aura of confidence that added to his overall appeal.

Of course, Patrick Stafford had probably been born with swagger. Certainly he'd had it even in high school. Though she hadn't known him back then, she'd known who he was, because his mother was a Blake and the Blakes were the wealthiest family in Haven, Nevada. And Blake Mining was the town's single biggest employer— which made her wonder why he'd chosen to leave the family business to embark on this new venture. Not that she was going to ask. After all, his rationale had nothing to do with her reason for being at his ranch.

And though Brooke wasn't ordinarily the type of woman who got all tongue-tied or weak-kneed in the presence of a handsome man, she'd definitely felt a quiver of something low in her belly when Patrick looked at her. It had been a long time since she'd experienced such an immediate attraction to a man—eight years, in fact— and she was unnerved by her response to this man now. Thankfully, she was a lot older and wiser than she'd been eight years earlier, and she had a much better understanding of what was at stake.

So she pushed her personal observations of the rancher aside to focus on her task. When she was done, Ranger gently bumped her shoulder with his nose, as if to say *thank you*.

She rubbed her palm over his cheek. "You're very welcome. But try to remember—as tempting as unlatched gates might be, it's not safe to wander off on your own."

He blew out a breath, as if to sigh, and she smiled.

"Do you always talk to your patients?" Patrick asked curiously.

Brooke hadn't heard him return and started now at the sound of his voice, but she responded to the question without missing a beat.

"Always," she confirmed. "I mean, I'm no Doctor Dolittle, but I believe the animals understand my tone and intent if not the actual words."

"Ranger certainly seems to," he acknowledged. Then, offering the mug he carried, he added, "Your coffee."

"Oh, um, thanks."

She took the mug and lifted it to her lips. It was strong and hot, just the way she liked it, though she hadn't wanted the drink so much as she'd wanted him not hovering while she tended to the injured horse.

"I was wondering about something you said earlier," he commented now.

"I said a lot of things—and held a lot more back," she admitted.

He smiled, and *damn* if that smile didn't do funny things to her insides.

Older and wiser, she reminded herself.

And with so much more to lose.

"You said that you were more interested in Ranger than the man paying the bill," he said, as if to prod her memory.

"You're still going to get a bill," she promised.

"I would expect so," he said. "But are you at least a little bit interested?"

She frowned as she took another sip of coffee. "What?"

"Being 'more interested' in Ranger suggests you're still interested in me. Doesn't it?" he asked hopefully.

"I'm definitely interested in being paid," she told him. "But Larissa—the clinic manager—will send you the bill."

"You're sidestepping my question," he noted.

"Actually, I'm waiting for you to stop talking so I can give you instructions for Ranger's follow-up care."

He inclined his head, a silent invitation to her to continue.

"His dressing will need to be changed daily until the wound is healed," she told him. "Do you have any ichthammol ointment?"

"I'm not sure," he said.

"I'll leave some and add it to the bill," she decided.

"What about changing the dressing? Will you come back to do that?" he asked.

She shook her head. "That shouldn't be necessary."

"Let me rephrase," he said. "Can *you please* come back to do that?"

She was surprised by the request. "Do you have any

idea what it will cost to have me come back out here to change a bandage?"

"I don't care what it costs," he told her.

Of course he didn't.

And because he didn't, she shrugged. "In that case, I'll see you tomorrow."

"Thanks." His quick smile conveyed relief and gratitude. "And how about tonight?"

"He'll be fine tonight," she assured him.

"I wasn't asking for Ranger," he said. "I was asking if *I* could see you tonight."

"No."

"Just for a drink," he cajoled.

Then he smiled again—this time a deliberately slow and sensual curve of his lips that had undoubtedly melted the resistance of many other women. Thankfully, experience had immunized Brooke against such obvious ploys.

She hoped.

"Or dinner, if you prefer," he said, when she didn't immediately respond.

"No and no," she replied, wondering how it was possible that he didn't already have a date lined up. Because it wasn't only a Friday—it was Valentine's Day.

Not that the occasion was a big deal to Brooke. It didn't matter to her that she wouldn't get chocolates or flowers, because she would be spending the night with the most important guy in her life.

"Tomorrow, then?" he suggested as an alternative.

She was flattered. And flustered.

But definitely *not* interested.

She shook her head. "No."

Still, he wasn't dissuaded. "Are you seeing someone?"

"How is that any of your business?"

"I'm curious about my competition," he said.

"There's no competition," she told him. "I'm not dating anyone right now and I'm not interested in dating anyone, especially not a pretend cowboy who doesn't have the sense to latch a paddock gate."

"Ouch," he said, feigning hurt.

Or maybe his pride really was wounded.

She didn't imagine a man as handsome and wealthy as Patrick Stafford heard the word *no* very often.

And perhaps her response had been a little harsh, not to mention unprofessional.

Yes, it frustrated her that an innocent animal had paid the price for his mistake, and it annoyed her that even now he didn't seem to realize there could be lasting repercussions for Ranger as a result of the injury. But she knew as well as anyone that busy people sometimes missed little details.

An unlatched gate.

A loose stirrup.

An expired condom.

Each one had repercussions.

"I'm sorry," she said. "That was uncalled for and possibly unfair."

"If you were really sorry, you'd offer to buy me a drink," he said, adding a wink for good measure.

She was grateful he'd accepted her apology—and irritated by his inability to take a hint.

"I'm not going to do that," she said. "But I will give you the ichthammol ointment at cost."

"Of course, I have no idea what 'cost' is," he acknowledged.

"About thirty percent less than you'd pay at the feed store," she told him, as she returned her equipment to her pack and zipped it up.

"A bargain," he decided. "Maybe I could put those savings toward a meal at The Home Station with you."

"You really don't understand the word *no*, do you?"

"I understand the word," he assured her. "I just thought, since it's getting close to dinnertime and we both have to eat, we might as well eat together."

She glanced at her watch. "Actually, it *is* almost dinnertime, which means that I just might make it home in time to eat with Brendan for a change."

He frowned at that. "Who's Brendan?"

"My seven-year-old son."

Chapter Two

Well, *that* was an unexpected revelation.

Patrick took a mental step back. He didn't realize he'd taken an actual physical step, too, until she called attention to his instinctive reaction.

"Yeah, that's the usual response from guys like you," she said.

"What response? And what do you mean—guys like me?"

"The retreat," she said, answering only his first question.

He frowned. "What are you talking about?"

"You literally took a step back, as if the responsibilities of parenting might be contagious."

"I did not," he denied. Except he realized that he was

standing a little farther away from her now. "Or if I did, I didn't mean anything by it."

"It doesn't matter," she said dismissively. "At least now we both know where the other one stands."

"And where is it that you think I stand?"

"As far away from any potential complications as you can possibly get."

He wished he could deny it—or at least point out that she didn't know him or anything about him. But while he often used flattery and charm to convey his interest in a woman, he tried to always be honest, too. Although he'd dated a lot of different women in his thirty-two years, the one thing those women all had in common was that they were no more interested in a long-term relationship than he was. And even if he did meet someone who might make him reconsider, the ranch was his priority now and for the foreseeable future.

He didn't have the time or—to be perfectly honest— any interest in a committed relationship. And he sure as hell wasn't looking to be a stand-in father to someone else's kid, because that was a scenario that *screamed* "complication" to him.

And while Brooke Langley might be the sexiest female to cross his path in months, she wasn't what he wanted. Even if the pressure behind his zipper suggested otherwise.

"I was just…surprised," he finally responded. "And now I'm curious… Is your son's father from around here?" he asked, wondering if the man might be someone he knew.

"Brendan doesn't have a father."

His brows lifted at that.

"The man who contributed to his DNA has no interest in being a dad," she explained. "He made that perfectly clear when I told him I was pregnant."

"I'm sorry," he said automatically.

"There's no reason to be," she told him. "He got his freedom and I got Brendan. And since my work is finished here, I really do want to get home to him now."

"But you'll be back tomorrow?" he said, not really a question so much as a reminder.

"I'll be back tomorrow," she confirmed.

He nodded, already looking forward to seeing her again.

As much as she loved her job, Brooke always looked forward to the end of the day because she loved coming home to her little boy even more. From the very first moment he was placed in her arms, her heart had filled with so much love, she'd been certain it would burst right out of her chest.

It wasn't always easy being a single mom, but she never regretted her decision to keep her baby. Of course, she was fortunate to have the unwavering support of her parents—and the luxury of living with Brendan in the apartment above their detached garage. The space was a little on the small side, but plenty big enough for the two of them, with two bedrooms, a four-piece bath, a decent-size family room and a modest kitchen with a breakfast bar.

The kitchen was the focus of her thoughts now, as she tried to remember what ingredients she had to put together for a meal. She was pretty sure there was ground beef in the freezer, and tacos weren't only quick and easy, they were one of Brendan's favorites.

She thought wistfully, for just a moment, about Patrick's invitation to dinner. It would be nice to go out to a restaurant where someone else prepared the food and cleaned up afterward. Of course, if that was really what she wanted, she could take Brendan out to eat at Diggers' tonight. The occasional treat at the popular bar and grill was within her budget even if a meal at The Home Station was not.

She pulled into the driveway beside her parents' house and parked in her usual spot in front of the garage. But she headed to the main house rather than her own apartment, knowing her son would be there. His school bus stopped in front of the house and, when he got off it at the end of the day, he knew to go see Gramma if his mom's truck wasn't in the driveway.

Brooke entered her childhood home through the side door and sat on the bench in the mudroom to remove her boots and hang her coat before stepping into the kitchen, where her mother was at the stove, stirring something in a pan. Though Sandra Langley had recently celebrated her sixtieth birthday, she still looked like the bride she'd been in the photos taken on her wedding day. There were some discernible changes, of course, the most obvious being that she wore her hair much shorter now, in a chin-length bob. But the shiny auburn tresses were the same color they'd been back then (thanks to a little assistance from Wendy at the Clip 'N' Curl), and her dark brown eyes still sparkled with humor.

"Mmm," Brooke said, sniffing the air as she crossed the room to kiss her mother's cheek. "Something smells good."

"It doesn't smell like much of anything yet," Sandra remarked. "I'm only browning ground beef."

"Well, it smells good to me," she insisted.

"You worked through lunch again, didn't you?"

"The clinic was packed," she said.

"You need to eat," her mom admonished. "How can you take care of the animals if you don't take care of yourself?"

"I do eat," she said. "In fact, I'll eat whatever you're cooking, if we're invited to stay for dinner."

"Tacos," Sandra said. "And of course you're welcome to stay."

She grinned. "Were the tacos Brendan's suggestion?"

"He did mention that he hadn't had them in *for-ev-er.*" Her mother stretched out the word to emphasize it the way Brooke was sure her son had done.

"Which is why I'd planned to make them for him when we got home," she said.

"Now you don't have to," Sandra told her.

"You spoil us," Brooke said.

Her mom smiled. "It's a mother's prerogative to spoil her kids—and grandkids. And since your father isn't home yet, having the two of you here for dinner means I won't have to eat alone."

"Is Dad still at Whispering Pines?"

Sandra shook her head. "He was on his way home when he got a call from Frieda Zimmerman asking him to stop by and take a look at Cupcake."

Brooke huffed out a breath. "She came into the clinic with Cupcake today. I gave the cat a thorough exam and assured Mrs. Zimmerman there was nothing wrong with her pet aside from the fact that she's fourteen years old."

"And for all of the fourteen years that Frieda's had the cat, she's been taking her to your dad for care," her mom pointed out.

"Sometimes I wonder if inviting me to help out in his practice has been any help to Dad at all."

"Of course it has," Sandra assured her. "And your dad is so proud and excited to work with you."

"Unfortunately, his clients are a little less enthusiastic when I show up instead."

"Why do I get the feeling you're talking about someone other than Frieda Zimmerman?"

"I'll fill you in on all the details after I hear about Brendan's Valentine's Day party at school. Where is he?"

"In your dad's office, doing his homework."

"He loves sitting in Grandpa's big chair," Brooke acknowledged.

"I think he loves spinning in Grandpa's big chair," her mother said, smiling. "Just like you used to do when you were a kid."

Brooke leaned in and gave her mom a hug, then went to find her son.

As she made her way down the hall, she found herself reflecting again on her good fortune. She knew there was no way she could do what she did without the support of her family—especially her mother. Sandra had been there not only to offer support and advice throughout

Brooke's pregnancy, but she'd given up her part-time job as a vet tech after Brendan was born so that she could take care of her grandson while Brooke finished college.

Though Brendan was in school full-time now, Brooke found that she relied on her mother just as much now for support and advice. She had friends in town, of course, but motherhood, school and then work had caused their paths to diverge long ago. As a result, her mom was probably her closest friend and confidante.

Pausing outside the door of her dad's office, she peeked in to confirm that Brendan was in the big leather chair, spinning, his hands catching and releasing the edge of the desktop as leverage to keep the chair turning.

She stepped into the open doorway and fisted her hands on her hips.

It took three more complete circles before Brendan noticed her, but when he did, he immediately grabbed hold of the desk with both hands to stop his momentum. He cast his eyes down, his cheeks flushed with guilt—or maybe it was excitement that was responsible for the color.

"What does Gramma say to you about spinning in Grandpa's chair?" she asked him.

"Not to let Grandpa catch me doing it," he said.

"Oh, really?" Brooke had to press her lips together to hold back her smile.

When she was a kid, she'd been told—firmly and repeatedly—not to do it, but apparently there were different rules for grandchildren.

"Or you could *not* spin in the chair. Then you wouldn't have to worry about getting caught," she pointed out to him.

"But it's fun to spin," he said and tipped his head back to smile at her, showing off the gap between his teeth where he'd recently lost both his central incisors.

He'd been sad when the first one started to loosen, until he learned that he could leave his tooth under his pillow and the tooth fairy would exchange it for money. Since then, there had been a few times that she'd caught him trying to wiggle teeth that weren't loose. *Just checking* was always his ready excuse.

"How come you're late today?" he asked her now.

She lifted a hand to ruffle his shaggy mop of hair. "I had to stop by Mr. Sterling's ranch to check on an injured horse."

"Did you make him better?" Brendan asked.

With both a mother and grandfather in the business of caring for animals, it probably wasn't surprising that he was so instinctively kindhearted and empathetic. Or that he'd announced, shortly after his seventh birthday, his intention to be the next Dr. B. Langley.

Brooke knew it was likely he'd change his mind a dozen times before he went to college, but it pleased her to know that, at least right now, her little boy looked up to her and wanted to follow in her footsteps.

"I gave him some medicine and bandaged his wound, but it's going to take a little time before he's all better," she said, mentally crossing her fingers that the stallion would make a full and complete recovery. "How was your party?"

"It was great," he said. "I got a valentine from everyone in my class—and *two* from Livia and Ruby. Do you want to see them?"

"Of course I want to see them."

He reached into his backpack and pulled out a brown paper bag labeled with his name in carefully printed letters and decorated all over with glittery pink and red hearts. He turned the bag upside down over the desk to dump out the contents.

"That's a lot of valentines," Brooke said, biting her lip to keep from smiling.

"I know," he gleefully agreed and proceeded to go through the pile, one by one, reading the traditional catchphrases or silly jokes printed on each of the cards and then telling her who it was from. Thankfully there were only eighteen kids in his second-grade class.

When he was done and the valentines were all stuffed back in the bag, she noticed the page of math problems on the desk. "Miss Karen gave you homework today?"

"Yeah." He made a face. "Math."

"I thought you liked math." She propped a hip against the corner of the desk.

"But this is *bo-or-ring*," he said, drawing out the word for emphasis.

She glanced at the half-completed worksheet. "It might be boring but knowing how to count money is important."

"I know how to count money."

"Do you? Because you circled the two quarters as representing fifty cents."

"Two quarters is fifty cents," he said confidently.

"But that's not the only grouping of coins that adds up to fifty cents," she pointed out. "And the instructions say to circle *all the groups* of coins that add up to the total amount given."

Brendan studied the problem for a moment, then drew a second circle around the picture of five dimes and a third around the image showing a quarter with two dimes and five pennies.

"Good job," she told him. "Now I'm going to let you finish that up while I help Gramma get dinner ready."

"Are we staying for dinner?" he asked hopefully.

"That's the plan."

"Yes!" He added a fist pump for good measure. "Gramma's making tacos."

"I know," she said.

"I *love* tacos."

"I know that, too," she said and dropped a kiss on the top of his head before heading back to the kitchen.

As she passed the dining room, she spotted the vase of long-stemmed red roses set on top of a crocheted doily in the center of the antique table.

The first year her parents were married, Bruce had apparently bought a single red rose for Sandra, to symbolize their first Valentine's Day as husband and wife. The second year he'd bought two roses, then continued to add to the number each successive year, so Brooke didn't need to count the gorgeous red blooms to know there were thirty-seven stuffed into the vase this year.

It was a lovely tradition and reassured her that happily-ever-afters were possible, even if the prospect of her own continued to be elusive. Not that she was actually looking for one right now, because she had different priorities as a working single mom. But maybe…someday.

"So tell me about your day," Sandra urged, after Brooke had washed up and began grating the block of cheddar she'd taken out of the fridge.

"You mean the part where I had my credentials questioned at the Silver Star?"

Her mother frowned. "Who would dare question your credentials?"

"The new owner."

"Patrick Stafford bought Gus's place, didn't he?"

Brooke nodded. "Though I have to wonder why. The man obviously doesn't know the first thing about taking care of animals."

"He must know something," Sandra said. "After all, his family was raising cattle on Crooked Creek long before gold and silver were discovered in the hills."

"Well, he didn't know to make sure the paddock gate was latched, and his horses got out and one of them was injured."

Her mom winced in sympathy. "How bad was it?"

Because her mother had been a vet's wife for thirty-seven years and worked as a vet tech in her husband's clinic for a lot of that time, Brooke didn't hesitate to share the details of her assessment and treatment of the stallion.

"At least Patrick had the good sense to call someone qualified to provide medical attention," Sandra remarked.

"He thought he was calling Dad," Brooke reminded her.

"Did you take care of the injury?"

She nodded.

"So now he knows he can call you instead." Her mother's eyes took on a speculative gleam. "Or maybe he'll call you even if he doesn't need help with a sick or injured animal."

"Don't go there," Brooke urged.

"Why not? He's handsome, charming and—"

"And he's well aware of his own attributes," she interjected.

"Ahh," her mom said, understanding. "He already hit on you, didn't he?"

"Yeah, but it wasn't too hard to shut him down," Brooke said, as she dumped the grated cheese into a bowl. "All it took was mention of my seven-year-old son."

And though she hadn't been the least bit surprised by Patrick's instinctive reaction, she had been the teensiest bit disappointed. And that reaction *had* surprised her.

"There's no doubt how much you love Brendan, but you've got to stop using him as a shield," Sandra admonished.

Brooke frowned at that. "How is being up-front about my status as a single mother using my child as a shield?"

"Maybe it's more like a sword," her mom decided. "A preemptive attack against any expression of interest."

"If a guy's interest can be struck down that easily, he's not someone I want to be with."

"That's probably a fair point," Sandra allowed. "But one of these days you're going to meet someone who isn't so easily dissuaded."

"I hope I do," she said.

But she already knew that Patrick Stafford wasn't that man.

So why was she looking forward to seeing him again?

Chapter Three

Patrick had gone off to college with the security of knowing there would be a job for him at Blake Mining as soon as he graduated. He'd never anticipated that, after only six years—and five different jobs—he'd feel trapped within the walls of his executive office. Or that he'd impulsively decide to walk away from the family business and buy a failing cattle ranch.

But that was what he'd done and, for the past four months, he'd lived and breathed the Silver Star. He'd known what changes and improvements he'd wanted to make, and he'd spent a lot of hours and even more money making them. He was determined to ensure the ranch was a success, to prove—to himself as much as his parents—that he could make it on his own in the real world. During that time, he'd been too busy to venture into town looking for female companionship—and likely too exhausted to do anything if he'd found it.

But he was starting to feel pretty good about the progress he'd made, pleased with the way everything was finally starting to come together. Or he had been until Dr. Brooke Langley called him a pretend cowboy and blamed him for Ranger's injury.

And *damn it*, she was right. If he'd latched the gate properly, the horses wouldn't have been running wild and the stallion wouldn't have been hurt. But her blunt assessment didn't just add to the weight of guilt he was already feeling; it rekindled his own doubts, further fueled by the incessant questions and criticisms of his parents, who were none too happy about his decision to leave Blake Mining and "play at being a rancher."

Maybe he was making a mistake. Maybe he would someday regret putting so much time and effort into the ranch. But that day wasn't today, and he'd come too far to back down now. He wasn't just invested but committed, and wouldn't the sexy vet be surprised to hear him confess that?

Except that he had to stop thinking of Brooke as the sexy vet and start remembering that she was a woman with serious responsibilities. A sexy single mom.

A mom he'd like to—

Whoa!

He immediately put a tight rein on *that* wayward thought.

No way was he going there.

Instead, he decided to go into town to grab a bite,

maybe have a couple of drinks, and clear all thoughts of the lovely Brooke Langley from his mind.

He wasn't looking for company when he took a seat at the bar at Diggers' Bar & Grill. And if he'd realized it was February 14, he likely wouldn't have ventured into town. But since he was here—and hungry—he ordered a draft and a pound of hot wings.

He'd taken the first sip of his beer when a curvy blonde hopped up onto the stool beside him and nudged her shoulder against his. "Hey there, handsome."

"Trinity, hi." He'd met the dental hygienist at a Fourth of July barbecue hosted by mutual friends a few years back, and they'd immediately hit it off. They'd had some good times together before going their separate ways, and when their paths had crossed again several months later, they'd enjoyed getting reacquainted.

They'd repeated the same song and dance a few more times after that, though the last time he'd seen her, she'd told him that she was dating somebody and thought he might be *the one*. Though Patrick wasn't sure he believed in such things, he'd been happy for Trinity and wished her the best.

He glanced past her now, looking for the man who'd been her constant companion in recent months. "Where's Christopher?"

Her easy smile wavered. "We broke up three weeks ago."

"I'm sorry." His response was both automatic and sincere.

"Me, too. It sucks to be alone on Valentine's Day."

Skylar Gilmore, working the bar, set Patrick's order

of wings down, then asked Trinity, "What can I get you?"

"Hendrick's gin and tonic with two lime wedges and half a twist of lemon."

The order didn't surprise Patrick—Trinity had always been high-maintenance, but he suspected that behind Sky's smile, the bartender was rolling her eyes.

"You can add that to my tab," Patrick said, when Sky set the G&T in front of Trinity.

The bartender nodded.

"Thanks, but I'm not the type of woman to go home with a man just because he buys me a drink—you'll have to share some of those wings, too," Trinity said with a wink.

"I'm happy to share." He nudged the plate toward her. "But I'm not looking to take anyone home tonight."

Trinity seemed puzzled by his response. "Nobody goes to a bar on Valentine's Day because they want to be alone."

"To be honest, I didn't even realize it was Valentine's Day until I got here and saw the Sweetheart Specials on the menu," he told her.

She selected a wing from his plate, bit into it. "So how are things at the Silver Star?"

"Pretty good," he said, because he was trying to forget about Ranger's injury and he definitely didn't want to discuss it with Trinity. She was firmly in his parents' camp, disapproving of his decision to walk away from a lucrative office job to live the life of a cowboy.

"You don't think you're going to miss working at Blake Mining with your family?" she pressed.

"I'm looking forward to the challenge of something different," he said. Because he'd never admit to anyone, except maybe his sisters, that he'd been looking for a way out for the past couple of years—and he was so glad to have finally found it.

"Is that why you're done with me?" she asked.

"You were done with me first," he reminded her. "As soon as you met Christopher."

"Because he told me he was looking to settle down and start a family," she said. "At least you were always honest about what you wanted and didn't want."

"And what I want hasn't changed."

"But what I want has—at least for tonight." She dropped the chicken wing bone in the bowl and lifted her hand to her mouth to lick sauce off her thumb. Then she drew it into her mouth, holding his gaze as she sucked on the digit.

It was a deliberately provocative action and one that would likely have piqued his interest at any other point in time. But tonight…nothing.

Because tonight he couldn't stop thinking about Brooke.

When Brooke woke up Saturday morning, she found Brendan already settled in front of the television with a bowl of cold cereal in his lap. She marveled over the ability of his internal alarm clock to unerringly shift between weekdays and weekends. Monday through Friday, it was a struggle to wake him in the morning. But on Saturdays, her son was always out of bed at the crack of dawn to watch his favorite cartoons on TV.

It was a routine she was happy to share with him whenever she had a Saturday off from the clinic. And since today was one of those days, Brooke got herself a bowl of Frosted Flakes, poured milk over her cereal and carried her breakfast to the living room to sit on the sofa beside her son. But as she chewed, she had the feeling there was something else she was supposed to be doing.

Or maybe she was just anticipating, because even when she wasn't scheduled to work at the clinic, there was always the possibility that she'd get called in to deal with an emergency—or called out to one of the local ranches, as had happened yesterday. And though the calendar was blank—save for the notation to check on Ranger sometime later in the day—and her phone remained silent, she couldn't shake the feeling.

When she and Brendan were both finished eating, she set their empty bowls aside. He snuggled closer to her side then and tipped his head back to smile at her.

Being a mom wasn't always easy, but it was always worthwhile. Sure, it might be nice to have a partner to share her life, but she'd rather be alone than with a man who couldn't understand and respect that her son had to be her number one priority right now.

She rarely wasted any time thinking about Brendan's father anymore, because the boy she'd fallen in love with in her second year of vet school had stopped being relevant to her a long time ago. But every once in a while— or when someone else brought up the subject (and, yes, that was another strike against Patrick Stafford)—she found herself wondering how any man could walk away from his child. But for the most part, she focused her attention and efforts on being the best mom she could be, so that Brendan wouldn't think about the fact that he didn't have a dad—and wouldn't feel as if he was missing out even if he did think about it.

Brooke knew her son had a couple of friends at school who also lived with only one parent, so his situation wasn't really unique. Except that each of Mason's and Felipe's living arrangements had changed after their respective parents divorced, and each of the boys still had both parents in their lives. So she had no doubt the day would come when Brendan asked why he didn't spend weekends with his dad like Mason and Felipe did with theirs. She just didn't know how she'd answer when it did.

"Did you finish your math homework last night?" she asked, when a commercial flashed across the screen.

He nodded. "Uh-huh."

"Did you double-check your answers?"

He nodded again.

"Did you leave it on Grandpa's desk?"

He threw his head back and slapped a hand against his forehead—a dramatic confirmation that, yes, he'd done that, too.

She chuckled. "We'll make sure we get it back before Monday."

"Maybe we can go get it after this show," he suggested.

"Are you worried we might forget about it?"

"No," he admitted. "I was hoping Grandpa would make pancakes."

"You just had breakfast," she reminded him.

"We could have pancakes for lunch."

"I could have made you pancakes if you'd really wanted pancakes," she said.

"Yeah, but Grandpa's pancakes are better."

She chuckled softly and hugged him close. "You're nothing if not honest, aren't you?"

"You told me I should always tell the truth."

"I did and you should," she agreed.

"So can we go to Gramma and Grandpa's?" he asked hopefully.

"Actually, I thought you might want to come to the Silver Star with me today."

"What's that?"

"It's the new name of Mr. Sterling's ranch."

"Why's it got a new name?" Brendan asked.

"Because Mr. Sterling sold the ranch to Mr. Stafford and moved to Glendale, Arizona."

"How come?"

She didn't think it was an appropriate time to get into a detailed discussion about economic downturns or retirement-age ranchers opting to sell off their properties because their kids had no interest in carrying on the family tradition. Instead she only said, "He wanted to move to a warmer climate."

"Why's it warmer in Arizona?"

"Because it's farther south and closer to the equator." She reached for the world atlas on the bottom shelf of the coffee table.

Brendan rolled his eyes. "You know you can get maps on the iPad, don't you?"

"Yes, I know," she confirmed. "But I want you to learn that you can find information in books, too."

"Why?"

"In case the internet blows up."

His eyes grew wide, conveying horror at the very thought. "Could that really happen?"

"Probably not," she acknowledged, opening the book and flipping through the pages until she found the double-spread illustration of the United States. "But we do sometimes lose our Wi-Fi connection."

"And that sucks," he said.

"That's the great thing about books—they don't need Wi-Fi." She tapped the page, drawing his attention to the map. "Do you know where we live?"

He immediately pointed to Nevada.

"That's right. But Haven is in northern Nevada," she said and nudged his finger closer to the state's top boundary. "And this—" she guided his finger down to Arizona "—is where Mr. Sterling lives now."

"That doesn't seem so far," Brendan decided.

"Scale can be hard to understand," she acknowledged. "Do you remember how long it took us to get to Disneyland last year?"

He nodded. *"For-ev-er."*

She smiled. "I'm sure it felt like forever, but it was actually about ten hours, split over two days. And this—" she pointed to Anaheim on the map "—is where Disneyland is."

His brow furrowed as he tried to equate the distance on the map with the hours in the car. "So Arizona is really, really far away," he realized.

"It is," she confirmed.

"Is that why he left his horses? Because they wouldn't want to be stuck in a trailer for a long trip like that."

She was always impressed by her son's innate understanding of and natural empathy toward animals, and she was both pleased and proud to know that he wasn't just a great kid but a compassionate human being. "That's probably one of the reasons," she agreed. "So do you want to go see the horses with me?"

Brooke ignored the echo of her mother's admonishment in her head. Because she knew that her motivation for inviting Brendan was that he enjoyed tagging along on official vet visits, just as she'd enjoyed tagging along with her father when she was a similar age.

She absolutely was not using her son as a shield—though she acknowledged, if only to herself, that she wouldn't object if Brendan provided a bit of a buffer. Because being in close proximity to Patrick Stafford made her tingle in places she hadn't thought were capable of tingling anymore.

"Would we go before or after Tanner's birthday party?" Brendan asked her now.

Birthday party?

And suddenly she remembered what she'd forgotten…

When Brooke pulled up at the Silver Star after dropping Brendan at Adventure Village for the birthday party, there were two vehicles in the driveway ahead of her. One was the same black F-150 that she recognized from the previous day; the other was an unfamiliar pale blue Land Rover.

Apparently the ranch's new owner had company, she mused, as she parked her dark green pickup behind Patrick's truck. Before she could speculate any further, the front door of the house opened and he stepped out onto the porch.

For a brief moment, she thought maybe he'd been waiting and watching for her. Then she realized he wasn't alone and probably wasn't even aware of her arrival, as his arm was slung casually across the shoulders of a gorgeous blonde who tipped her head back and laughed at whatever he said to her.

Well, it certainly hadn't taken him long to bounce back from her rejection the day before. Which proved that she'd pegged him right from the beginning and that her long-dormant hormones had come out of hibernation at the wrong time and for the absolute wrong guy.

She climbed out of her truck as the other woman gave Patrick a quick hug, then skipped down the steps. She wore a long black coat unbuttoned over a short scarlet-red dress paired with knee-high boots with chunky heels. Not just gorgeous but stylish, Brooke noted.

The blonde opened the driver's-side door of her vehicle, but before getting in, she called out to Patrick over the roof: "By the way, I left a toothbrush in the bathroom. Don't you dare throw it out."

If Brooke had any doubts about the woman's reason for being at the ranch, that parting remark answered them. Obviously she'd spent the night and expected to be back for a repeat performance.

Patrick didn't respond to his departing guest's comment, but he watched as the SUV zipped down the driveway and disappeared from sight before he moved off the porch.

"I didn't expect you'd be here this early," he said, falling into step with Brooke as she made her way toward the barn.

"I didn't think it was particularly early, but I'm sorry if I showed up at an inopportune time," she said.

He pulled open the barn door. "Why would you think it's an inopportune time?"

She gestured to the driveway, though the blonde and her Land Rover were long gone.

"Oh, you don't have to worry about Jenna," he said dismissively. "She has a habit of overstaying her welcome, but she's mostly harmless."

Brooke was so stunned by his callous remark, it took her a moment to come up with a reply. "If that's a recurring problem, maybe you should consider sleeping at her place," she suggested coolly, as she made her way to Ranger's stall. "That way you could leave whenever you wanted."

It was an effort to bank down on her irritation so the horse wouldn't pick up on her mood, but she managed to do so and turned her attention to the stallion. Using her voice and her touch to remind him of her presence and her purpose, she opened the gate and stepped inside his enclosure with his halter and lead in hand.

She was pleased—and maybe a little surprised—to discover that Ranger's stall had been freshly mucked out. Either Patrick hadn't spent all morning lounging in bed with his companion or he'd hired someone to perform basic chores. Considering his willingness to pay the cost of a site visit for her to change Ranger's dressing, she suspected it was probably the latter. Either way, it reassured her that—the stallion's injury notwithstanding—the animals at the Silver Star were being cared for.

"What are you talking about?" Patrick asked now, sounding sincerely baffled.

She glanced at him as she led Ranger to the treatment area.

The rancher was standing with his arms folded, a scowl furrowing his brow.

"I was just providing a solution to your girlfriend dilemma."

"Girlfriend?" he echoed blankly.

"I'm sorry—does that word carry too much meaning for you?" she asked, as she secured the stallion's ties. "I wasn't sure how else to refer to the woman who made a point of mentioning that she'd left her toothbrush in your bathroom."

He shook his head. "Not *my* bathroom. The guest bathroom."

"Oh, well, that's completely different, then," she remarked dryly.

Patrick no longer seemed confused. Now he looked amused. "I think you've misread the situation."

"It's really none of my business," she acknowledged. "My only purpose here is to take care of your horse. If you want to watch and learn, I'd be happy to explain what I'm doing. If you don't, please stop talking so I can give Ranger my complete attention."

He stopped talking, but he didn't leave, as she'd hoped he might do, and she felt his gaze on her the whole time.

When she'd completed her task and returned the horse to its stall, she took a small apple out of her pocket and offered it to the stallion—a reward for his good behavior. Ranger gently plucked the fruit from her hand and crunched down on the treat.

With a last pat on his cheek, Brooke turned around and found herself face-to-face with Patrick again.

"You misread the situation," he said, picking up the conversation where they'd left off.

"It's none of my business," she said again.

"True," he acknowledged. "But Jenna isn't my girlfriend. She's my sister."

"Your…sister?" she echoed, suddenly feeling foolish.

Because replaying his comment in her mind now, she realized the words that sounded like a callous dismissal of a lover could also be—and apparently were—the lighthearted teasing of a sibling.

"I have two of them," he told her. "Jenna's the youngest. She was at dinner with her boyfriend last night when he got called into work."

"On Valentine's Day?"

"Nate works at a tech company that does a lot of government work, and a break-in at the office meant that everyone had to go in. Anyway, that's how Jenna ended up at Diggers' after she finished the romantic dinner for two by herself and, because she didn't want to go home to an empty apartment, she decided to come back here."

"Oh."

"You could apologize now," he suggested.

"I apologize for jumping to conclusions," she said,

not just sincerely regretful but embarrassed by her un-characteristically emotional reaction to the situation.

"And for impugning my character?"

"Actually, you should be flattered I imagined you could ever get a woman as gorgeous as your sister."

He chuckled at that, but his expression quickly turned serious again. "You don't have a very favorable opinion of me, do you?"

"I don't know you."

"And yet you were quick to assume that, only hours after you'd turned down my invitation for drinks and/or dinner yesterday, I'd go out and pick up another woman."

She shrugged. "There was no reason why you shouldn't."

"You're right," he acknowledged. "And the truth is, I did go out last night...but you're the reason I came home alone. Because the whole time I was at the bar, I couldn't stop thinking about you."

"I have a child," she reminded him.

"Yeah, you mentioned that," he said.

But this time, instead of moving away, he moved closer.

"And I have no interest in being the next notch on your bedpost," she said, determined to firmly establish the boundaries between them.

"I bought a new bed when I moved in here—there are no notches. In fact, there aren't even posts."

"I think you missed my point."

"It might not be what either of us expected, but there's definite chemistry between us," he said and lifted a hand to lightly stroke her cheek with the backs of his knuckles.

It was a gentle touch, but there was something so sensual about the caress that she found herself wondering how his hands might feel on other parts of her body.

On *every* part of her body.

And the wondering made her blood heat and her heart pound.

She swallowed. "I don't believe in chemistry."

"No?" His lips curved in a knowing smile. "Then explain to me why I can see the pulse point at the base of your jaw racing."

"Because you're crowding me, and I don't like to be crowded."

He immediately took a step back, giving her the space she'd claimed she wanted.

But then he asked, "How about being kissed?" And the low timbre of his voice was every bit as seductive as his touch. "Do you like being kissed?"

How could she answer that question when she could hardly remember how it felt to be kissed?

Oh, she got lots of kisses from her little boy, and she loved every one of them—even the wet and sticky ones. She also regularly exchanged pecks on the cheek with her parents. But she honestly couldn't recall when she'd last been kissed by a man.

And with Patrick's lips so temptingly close, she realized that she desperately wanted to answer his question.

Whether yes or no, she wanted to know how it felt to be kissed by this man. She wanted to know the taste of his lips and the touch of his hands. And even though she knew it might turn out to be a very big mistake, the wanting was suddenly stronger than her determination to resist.

"I'll let you know," she said and breached the short distance between them to press her mouth against his.

Chapter Four

Brooke's impulsive action had been fueled by curiosity. Would his kiss curl her toes inside her boots? Would it make her blood race through her veins? Would she feel the flutter of wings in her belly as butterflies soared?

Or would the experience be a disappointment, her excited anticipation unfulfilled?

It had been a long time since she'd experienced feelings of physical attraction—and even longer since she'd felt anything as immediate and intense as what she'd felt the first time she came face-to-face with Patrick Stafford less than twenty-four hours earlier.

And now she was kissing this man she'd only just met, and she was not disappointed.

Not just kissing him but pressing herself against him,

desperate to get closer. Apparently that was what eight years of abstinence did to a woman.

Or maybe it really was the inexplicable chemistry he'd mentioned that was responsible for her actions. She'd tried to ignore the tension between them, refusing to acknowledge that there even was an attraction. And while she couldn't deny that her pulse accelerated whenever he was near and she had to lock her knees so they didn't tremble, she'd mostly managed to ignore her body's instinctive response to his nearness.

Until he'd been too close for her to ignore.

Too close to resist.

But in the first moment that their mouths met, Brooke realized that she'd made a tactical mistake. Because in that first moment, a blast of unexpected heat flooded her system, melting her bones, making her weak.

Making her want.

She curled her fingers into his jacket, holding on to him as the intensity of the need shook her to the core. And that was before his tongue slid between her lips, stroking the inside of her mouth, stoking the fire that burned in her belly and spread through her veins. Before his hands slid up her back, drawing her still closer to the solid strength of his body.

Even through the layers of clothing and outerwear between them, she felt her breasts rub against the hard wall of his chest, her nipples tightening into hard buds that ached to be acknowledged.

Touched.

Tasted.

She could all too easily envision his dark head bent

over her breast, his mouth closing around the turgid peak, and the explicit and arousing image nearly made her gasp.

It *did* make her pull away, in a determined effort to regain control of her runaway hormones.

Patrick seemed to need a minute, too, before he asked, "Is that a 'yes'?"

It took Brooke a moment longer to realize he was still waiting for a response to his earlier question. A question she could barely remember.

"Do you like kissing?" he prompted.

She pressed her tingling lips together. "It seems that I do," she finally responded, keeping her tone light so he wouldn't guess his kiss had set off a maelstrom inside her.

His smile was more than a little smug as he reached for her again, but she took a quick step back this time and held up a hand.

"You just admitted that you like kissing," he pointed out. "And I really want to kiss you again."

Brooke was flattered by his interest, but she was also wary. One kiss had been enough to nearly wipe her mind clean of all rational thought, unleashing such a surge of desire through her system that she could focus on nothing else. And she needed to focus.

She was a woman with obligations and responsibilities of a kind he didn't want to know. So she couldn't allow herself to get caught up in the heat of the moment, because she knew she'd end up getting burned.

"I also like Sweet Caroline's Twelve-Layer Chocolate Bliss," she said lightly. "But I know I can't have it every day."

"I'm flattered that you equated kissing me with the best chocolate cake in the county, but I have to disagree with your premise on two grounds," he said. "First, a small piece of Chocolate Bliss every day wouldn't do any harm. In fact, it's widely believed that an occasional indulgence curtails the impulse to binge. Second, kissing—even *not* in moderation—isn't harmful to your health, and studies have shown that people who share kisses every day live longer and happier lives."

She narrowed her gaze. "You just made that up."

"Even if I did, I bet I could find such a study."

"And probably also a study that proves the opposite," she argued.

"You're a cynic, I see," he said, sounding amused.

"A realist," she countered.

"Science has proved that the endorphins released during sexual activity are natural mood boosters and stress relievers," he said.

"Well, aren't you just a font of self-serving information? But as much as I appreciate the chemistry lesson, I'm a single mom," she reminded him. "I have neither the time for nor any interest in having an affair."

"I think you're interested, but there's something holding you back. Tell me what it is, what you're afraid of."

"I'm not afraid of anything except my own bad judgment when it comes to the male species," she said. "So while I did enjoy our kiss, it won't happen again."

"That's too bad." He sounded sincerely regretful. "Because I think we'd be really good together."

He might be right, but she knew from experience that the temporary pleasure wouldn't be worth the heartache that followed. "I have no doubt you could sell that line to any number of women, but I'm not buying."

"Could I at least buy you a cup of coffee?" he suggested as an alternative. "A fresh pot just finished brewing when you pulled up."

As much as she wanted to make her escape, she needed to reestablish the professional boundaries of their relationship and decided that a discussion of neutral topics over a cup of coffee might help do that.

"Coffee sounds good," she decided and followed him out of the heated barn and into the frigid outdoors.

She detoured to her truck, to set her backpack inside, then fell into step with him again as he headed toward the main house.

Inside, he shrugged out of his leather jacket and hung it on a hook, then held out a hand for hers, hanging it beside his own.

"Don't worry about your boots," he said, when she started to reach down.

Since he obviously wasn't worried about his, she followed him into the kitchen.

She briefly wondered if she was crossing a line by entering his home, but immediately dismissed the concern. In rural practice, it was common for clients to become friends. She'd certainly never questioned the lines when she had a cup of tea with Stasia Krecji or accepted a bag of homemade lemon cranberry muffins from Betty Andersen. But she'd also never kissed Stasia or Betty, so maybe it was the lingering effects of the lip-lock she'd shared with Patrick Stafford that was causing her to question the placement of the lines now.

Maybe? her conscience mocked.

Brooke ignored the nagging voice to focus on her surroundings.

When she'd learned that the new owner of Gus Sterling's property intended to turn it into a dude ranch, she'd wondered about the changes that might be made to the homestead. Some of those changes—such as the new logo on the barn and the upgraded fencing around the paddocks—had been immediately evident when she'd pulled into the driveway the day before. But the two-story log home appeared unaltered from the outside.

Looking around the kitchen now, she was pleased to see that Gus's natural-stained maple cabinets remained, though the scarred and chipped laminate countertops had been replaced by dark granite. An island had been installed where the former owner's pedestal table and chairs had previously sat, and the high-end appliances were obviously new.

Patrick opened a cupboard beside the coffee maker and retrieved two mugs, then filled both with coffee and handed one to Brooke.

"Have a seat," he invited, gesturing to the four stools lined up at the island.

She accepted the mug and sat.

Patrick remained standing on the other side of the island, facing her.

"Do you cook?" she asked, eyeing the six-burner cooktop and double ovens. "Or are you planning to hire someone to prepare meals for your guests?"

"I suspect paying guests will expect a little more variety and substance than I can manage, so I'll hire someone," he said.

"If you don't mind my asking, what made you decide to walk away from an executive position at Blake Mining to take on something like this?"

It was a question Patrick had been asked by more than a few people after he'd tendered his resignation, and one he still wasn't entirely sure how to answer.

"I wanted a change," he replied, because it was true if not the whole truth.

"So you're just a spoiled little rich boy playing at being a rancher?" she mused, the teasing tone taking the sting out of her words.

"I can't deny the spoiled or rich part," he said. "But I'm neither little nor a boy."

"Spoiled big rich man, then," she noted.

"And I'm not playing at anything. This ranch isn't a whim or a hobby, though my parents have occasionally labeled it as both," he acknowledged. "It's my new life."

"What was wrong with your old life?" she asked curiously.

"Too much money and too little responsibility."

"Said no one ever," Brooke chimed in.

"I know it sounds strange," he admitted. "And maybe there will come a day that I want to go back to Blake Mining, where I'm expected to occupy a chair at board meetings but not actually have an opinion about anything—or worse, dare to express it."

"Was it really so bad?"

"Probably not," he allowed. "But the more time I spent there, the more I realized that I didn't want to spend the rest of my life there."

"But why a dude ranch?" she wondered.

"It's a vacation ranch," he said. "And truthfully, the idea wasn't even mine. It kind of came out of the blue as a result of me being late for the bachelor party of one of my college friends. When I explained that I'd been helping my grandfather brand the new calves at Crooked Creek, my buddies all started ribbing me about playing cowboy. So of course I said they only wished they had the same opportunity to escape their boring corporate jobs every once in a while, which led to a surprisingly coherent and meaningful conversation about the conflict between making a living and having a life.

"Anyway, it was Josh who said that when it was time for his bachelor party, instead of getting drunk and losing his money in Vegas, he wanted us all to go to a dude ranch."

"You bought Gus Sterling's ranch in order to host your buddy's bachelor party?" she asked incredulously.

He chuckled. "No. Josh wasn't even dating anyone at the time, so his bachelor party wasn't—and isn't—anywhere on the horizon. But his comment did get me thinking. After all, I knew a little bit about ranching, a little bit more about business, and I had available funds to invest in a new venture." He shrugged. "So when I heard that Gus was looking to sell, I took it as a sign that the time was right to pursue a career change."

"I would expect someone who buys a ranch to know more than a little bit about ranching," she noted.

"I knew enough to keep on Levi and Dean to look after the cattle."

She nodded, obviously recognizing the names of Gus Sterling's longtime ranch hands.

"They have more than forty combined years of experience and have probably forgotten more about cattle than I could ever hope to know," he continued.

"What would you have done if they'd wanted to move on when Gus sold?" Brooke asked.

"I probably would have considered selling the herd," he admitted. "Except that a cattle ranch without cattle isn't likely to draw many visitors."

"Not likely," she agreed.

"But Gus had good stock that I felt confident would do well with guests of various levels of experience and could be used for ranch work as well as on trails and for riding lessons. Which is one of the reasons I felt so awful when I realized Ranger was injured," he confided to her now.

"I know I gave you a hard time about the unlatched gate, but the truth is, coronary band injuries are quite common and can have any number of causes."

He nodded. "But I also know his injury is more severe than is common."

"He's going to need some time to heal," she said.

"And the attentive care of a good vet," he added.

"In coordination with the farrier," she said. "Gavin Torres is out of town this weekend, but he promised to stop by on Monday to check on Ranger and assess long-term options."

"You think there's going to be permanent damage," he realized.

"Damage to the coronary band usually results in slow and abnormal hoof growth, but it doesn't necessarily affect the animal's mobility or utility. Once it's healed, Gavin will be able to determine the best method to support the hoof during regrowth and give your stallion the best chance for a complete recovery."

Before his mind could wander too far down that dark path, she shifted the conversation again.

"It takes a lot of courage to step outside your comfort zone and try something new," she said. "And I really hope the ranch works out for you."

"Thanks. Of course, I do have a job waiting for me at Blake Mining if it doesn't," he pointed out.

"And now I'm a little less impressed," she said, but tempered the words with a smile.

"What about you?" he asked. "What made you want to become a vet?"

"I'm not sure," she admitted. "I only know that it's what I always wanted to do, and I feel grateful every day that I'm lucky enough to do it."

"I'm sure achieving your goal had more to do with hard work than good luck."

"There was a lot of hard work," she agreed.

"So maybe it's time to let yourself have a little bit of fun," he suggested.

"Is *fun* supposed to be some kind of code for *sex*?" she asked dubiously.

"Sex *is* fun if you do it right," he said.

She shook her head. "Unfortunately, I'm too busy with real responsibilities to have time for a fling with a pretend cowboy."

When he'd decided to make a drastic career change, he'd known that he'd need to prove himself, so he wasn't offended by her characterization. He was more than a little disappointed, though, by her determination to fight the obvious chemistry between them. "That is unfortunate," he agreed.

"And speaking of time—" Brooke glanced at the watch on her wrist "—I need to go if I'm not going to be late picking up Brendan."

She lifted her mug to her lips to swallow the last mouthful of coffee, then set the cup down again and pushed her stool away from the counter.

"Where is he?" Patrick asked.

"A birthday party for one of his classmates."

He didn't try to persuade her to stay even a little while longer. Though he might not have the same type of responsibilities, he understood and respected her priorities.

"I'll walk you out," he said.

After he'd done so, Patrick stood on the driveway and watched Brooke's truck grow smaller and smaller until it finally disappeared from his sight, with only one thought in his mind: he never should have kissed her.

Although technically she'd kissed him, he'd practically goaded her into it.

He'd been wondering about the taste of her sweetly curved lips since their first meeting, but instead of satisfying his curiosity, the feel of her mouth against his had only stoked his desire.

A desire that he suspected no other woman could satisfy.

He wasn't accustomed to being preoccupied by any one woman—especially a woman who'd made it clear that she wasn't interested.

Except that her enthusiastic participation in their kiss proved her claim of disinterest was a lie.

Brooke Langley *was* interested, even if she didn't want to be.

And he knew exactly how that felt.

Because she might be the hottest woman he'd met in a long time, but she wasn't at all his type. Not because he didn't like long-legged redheads, but because he didn't like complications.

So why, even knowing about her child, couldn't he get her out of his mind? What was it about her that appealed to him? Was it the challenge she presented? Was he so accustomed to getting what he wanted that he didn't know how to accept rejection?

Or was it simply that the kiss had affected him more deeply than he wanted to admit?

Because, really, that was all it had been—a simple kiss.

Except that there was nothing simple about the way she'd felt when she was in his arms.

Brendan apparently had a great time at Tanner's birthday party, and he talked nonstop the whole way home about everything the party guests had done at

Adventure Village—"we played three games of laser tag *and* got four tokens for the video games"—the cake Tanner's mom had made—"it had, like, six layers, and each one was a different color"—and all the goodies in his loot bag—"a yo-yo and a super bouncy ball and a slinky and stickers and bubble gum and a *gi-nor-mous* lollipop."

Brooke was glad for his incessant chatter because it meant she wasn't expected to contribute much to the conversation. An occasional murmur of agreement or expression of awe was enough to keep her son talking, if not quite enough to alleviate her feelings of guilt.

And she did feel guilty. Not just because her son was only getting a fraction of her attention or even because she'd kissed Patrick, but because—more than an hour and a half later—she couldn't stop thinking about the kiss.

She never should have let it happen, because now that they'd shared one kiss, she wanted more. Not just more kisses but more of everything that came after the kissing.

For the better part of eight years, she hadn't regretted not having a man in her life. She certainly hadn't felt as if she was missing out on anything, because she had her little boy and he made her life complete so that she didn't need anything or anyone else. Or so she'd believed.

But now, after sharing only one kiss with Patrick, she found herself suddenly feeling a little less satisfied with her life. A little less complete. And she couldn't help but wonder: What was it about the man that urged her to step outside her comfort zone? What was it about him that made her want more?

He'd asked what she was afraid of, and she'd told him she wasn't afraid. But it was a lie. She was terrified of the way she felt when she was near him. The way her blood pulsed and her knees quivered; the way her blood heated and her body yearned.

She'd felt a similarly intense desire once before—eight years earlier. She'd fallen hard and fast for Xander Davis, and had her heart broken into a million little pieces as a result. Still, she'd never wished she could go back or change a single thing about their brief and passionate relationship, because it had resulted in Brendan—and her son was truly her biggest accomplishment and her greatest joy.

But her relationship with Xander had also taught her some important lessons: that passion was fleeting, romantic love was an illusion and her judgment was hopelessly flawed when her hormones were engaged. So the fact that she'd responded to Patrick as immediately and intensely as she'd responded to Xander was a great big and wildly waving red flag.

She wasn't afraid of what might happen if she fell into bed with the wrong man, but she was afraid of what might happen if she fell in love with the wrong man again. And Patrick Stafford was, by his own admission, the wrong man.

Having an affair with him would be reckless and irresponsible. (And, if his kiss was any kind of indicator, an incredible and exquisite pleasure.)

So it was a good thing that Brooke was too level-headed and responsible to let herself get carried away by her own wanton desires again.

But when she went to bed later that night, her lips were still tingling from the aftereffects of his kiss.

Chapter Five

The following morning, Brooke and Brendan walked over to the main house for breakfast, her son having convinced his grandfather to make banana-chocolate-chip pancakes. Not that he'd required much convincing. Bruce absolutely doted on his only grandson and was always happy to indulge his requests.

In addition to the towering stack of pancakes, there was a platter of bacon and sausage and, while her dad was scrambling eggs—because apparently it wasn't breakfast without eggs, too—Brooke poured coffee and juice and set the table. She sometimes enlisted Brendan to help with the latter task, but as soon as they'd walked through the door, his grandmother had ushered him upstairs to go through a box of old toys that she'd found in the attic.

"Remind me again why I thought it was a good idea to move out," Brooke said, as she stole a sausage link from the platter.

"You said you needed to stand on your own two feet so that Brendan would learn to do the same," Bruce said. "And you were right."

"Of course, I'm standing on my own two feet only three hundred feet away most of the time," she acknowledged. "And in your kitchen the rest of the time."

Her dad chuckled. "You know we don't mind. In fact, it's nice for your mom and me to have other people around the table. After almost thirty-eight years of marriage, we run out of things to talk about sometimes."

"I know that's not true," Brooke said. "You guys are an amazing example of what a marriage should be, even after almost thirty-eight years."

"There is no *should*," Bruce said. "Every marriage is as different as the people in it. But I know I got lucky, not just with my wife but the kids we had together."

"Especially me, right?" Brooke teased. "Because I'm your favorite."

"You're my favorite daughter," her dad confirmed.

It was a familiar exchange between them, and Brooke was smiling as she began folding napkins for the table. But her mind started to wander, and she didn't realize her dad had spoken again until she heard her name.

"I'm sorry—did you say something else?"

"Nothing important," Bruce said, scraping the eggs out of the pan and into a bowl.

Brooke finished with the napkins, then retrieved the butter and syrup from the fridge.

"Is everything okay?" her dad asked. "You seem a little distracted this morning."

"Just thinking about the day ahead," she said.

It wasn't a lie, because she had been thinking about her impending trip to the Silver Star—and seeing Patrick again. And trying to get a grip on the array of emotions that churned inside her. Because thinking about the upcoming visit made her stomach knot with excitement and apprehension.

She had no doubt the kiss she'd shared with Patrick had meant more to her than it had to him, and undoubtedly more than it should. Especially because he wasn't interested in a woman with a child.

Except that he hadn't kissed her like a man who wasn't interested.

But maybe, in the heat of the moment, he'd forgotten her single-mom status. If so, she could hardly fault him, as her son had been the furthest thing from Brooke's mind at the time, too. In any event, she was glad that Brendan had decided he wanted to visit the ranch with her today. There was no way either she or Patrick would be able to forget her maternal responsibilities when Brendan was right there.

Bruce called his wife and grandson to breakfast before he asked Brooke, "What are your plans today?"

"Aside from a quick trip to the Silver Star, I'm hoping to do a whole lot of nothing."

Her dad frowned. "Are you really going to go out there just to change Ranger's dressing every day?"

"As long as that's what the client wants and he's willing to pay for my time," she confirmed.

When everyone was seated at the table with their plates loaded up with food, conversation shifted to what was on her parents' agenda for the day.

"We're heading out to the flea market," Sandra said.

Brooke wrinkled her nose. "I've never understood your fascination with flea markets."

In her opinion, they were too crowded and noisy and musty smelling, but her mother's eyes always lit up just like Brendan's did when he was in front of a candy counter.

"One woman's trash is another woman's treasure," Sandra said, paraphrasing.

"The 'another woman' being your mother," Bruce chimed in, with a wink.

"So it would seem," Brooke agreed.

"I'll have you know that your apartment was primarily furnished with flea-market finds," her mother pointed out.

Brooke knew it was true. Luckily Sandra had a knack for spotting quality materials and workmanship, even when buried beneath layers of cheap paint and unidentifiable grime. She also had the patience to strip and sand and restore, after which the finished product usually bore little resemblance to what she'd brought home from the market. Most recently she'd found an oversize coffee table that she was repurposing for Brendan's wooden train set.

"Can I go to the flea market, too?" Brendan asked hopefully, no doubt thinking about the bins of secondhand toys and boxes of comic books that he could sift through, because Gramma always let him choose one to bring home. On a recent trip he'd found a rare Batman comic for only twenty-five cents and now imagined himself to be a treasure hunter like his grandmother.

"Of course," Sandra replied.

At the same time Brooke said, "You wanted to go to the Silver Star with me today."

"Oh, right," he said, but he no longer sounded as happy about that plan as he'd been earlier.

"And if we're not there too long, maybe we can stop at Adventure Village for a game of mini golf," Brooke suggested, sweetening her offer.

"Yay!" he agreed, with decidedly more enthusiasm this time. "Or maybe laser tag?"

She had no objection to Brendan playing laser tag with his friends, but the high-energy game with loud music and flashing lights was not really her idea of a good time.

"You played three games of laser tag yesterday," she reminded him. "So your options are mini golf or home."

"Mini golf," he immediately agreed.

When everyone had finished eating, Bruce shooed his wife and daughter out of the kitchen so that he and Brendan could do the tidying up.

"Is there any particular reason you don't want Brendan to come to the flea market with us?" Sandra asked, when they were settled in the living room with their refilled mugs of coffee.

"It's not that I didn't want him to go with you but that I wanted him with me," Brooke clarified. "He was at Tanner's birthday party for most of the day yesterday, and I kind of missed hanging out with him."

"Are you sure that's all it is?" her mom pressed. "Your desire for Brendan's company has nothing to do with the fact that you're going to see Patrick Stafford today?"

It was both a blessing and a curse that her mother could read her so easily, Brooke mused, as she sipped her coffee and considered a response to the question.

"Maybe not nothing," she allowed.

Sandra's brow furrowed. "I know I was teasing you about him being a handsome man, but if he's said or done anything to make you feel at all uncomfortable about being alone—"

"No." Brooke shook her head, eager to reassure her mother. "It's just…you were right. He is handsome and charming, and maybe I'm not as immune as I want to believe. So, yes, having Brendan there will serve as a reminder *to me* about what can happen when a woman lets herself fall under the spell of a handsome and charming man."

"Okay," her mom said. "Because we could send your father to the Silver Star to tend to the horse and you and Brendan could come with me."

"Thanks, but no," Brooke said, aware that her reason for turning down the offer had little to do with her dislike of the flea market and a lot to do with a certain sexy rancher.

Though he would never admit it to anyone else, Patrick was watching for Brooke's arrival. Sure, he was sitting in front of his computer in the den, pretending to review the website design samples his cousin Devin had sent to him, but he was too distracted by thoughts of the sexy vet to note subtle differences in background colors and font styles, never mind form an opinion about them.

As much as he was looking forward to seeing Brooke again, he knew it would be a mistake to pursue a personal relationship with her. As she'd pointed out, she was too busy with real responsibilities to indulge in an affair with a pretend cowboy, and he wasn't in a position to offer her anything more. All things considered, the smart move would be to take a step back.

Of course, as soon as he saw her truck pull into the driveway, he pushed his chair away from the desk and went to put on his coat and boots so that he could meet her by the barn.

His lips automatically curved when she stepped out of the vehicle. Then he heard the back door open and shifted his gaze in time to see a little boy hop out. Her son, he guessed, his surprise yielding to amusement as he realized she'd likely brought the kid to act as a barrier between them, to ensure there would be no more earth-tilting kisses like the one they'd shared the day before.

And while he was admittedly a little disappointed, he was also encouraged, because she wouldn't have felt the need for a safeguard unless she'd been as affected by their kiss as he was.

"Good afternoon, Mr. Stafford," she said by way of greeting.

"Dr. Langley." He matched her formality with his response, then turned his attention to the boy who'd taken position by his mother's side. The top of the kid's head, covered in a red knit pom-pom cap, was level with her breasts, so Patrick estimated his height at around four feet. He was wearing a puffy royal blue ski jacket over jeans with cowboy boots on his feet. His hair—what was visible beneath the edges of his hat—was sandy brown and his eyes were dark blue and wide with curiosity.

"I'm guessing this is your son," he said to Brooke.

She nodded. "This is Brendan."

"Hello, Brendan," Patrick said and offered his hand for the boy to shake. "I'm Patrick."

"It's nice to meet you, Mr. Stafford," the boy politely replied.

"Mr. Stafford is my father," he said. "Patrick is fine,"

"My mom says using titles is a sign of respect," Brendan told him.

"Well, I would never want to disagree with your mom," Patrick said, fighting against the smile that wanted to curve his lips. "But maybe we can come up with an alternative that doesn't make me feel so old."

"How about Mr. Patrick?" Brendan suggested. "That's what we call the teachers at school."

His brows rose. "You call all your teachers Mr. Patrick?"

The boy giggled in response to Patrick's feigned misunderstanding. "My teacher is Miss Karen, the librarian is Mrs. Donna and the gym teacher is Mr. Grant," he explained.

"Ah." Patrick nodded his understanding, then looked at Brooke. "What do you think, Dr. Langley?"

"I think Mr. Patrick is acceptable," she agreed, then turned to her son again. "But the most important thing to remember is that you're not to bother Mr. Patrick while we're here."

"I won't," Brendan promised, as he followed his mother into the barn.

Brooke retrieved the stallion's halter and lead rope from the hook beside his door and stepped into the stall.

"He's big," Brendan said, taking an instinctive step back when the stallion exited the enclosure.

"He is big," Patrick confirmed. "And incredibly strong. That's why it's important to keep a safe distance."

"It's hard to examine an animal from a safe distance," the boy said matter-of-factly. "But I know to always approach a horse from the side to avoid his blind spots and to talk to him so he knows I'm there. My mom gives me the same lecture every time we visit one of the local ranches."

"How often is that?" Patrick asked.

"Almost every weekend, and some other days when I'm not at school. But if Mom knows she's gonna be a long time—or if she's gonna be doing something she doesn't want me to see—she makes me stay with Gramma."

"You don't like staying with Gramma?"

He shrugged. "I don't mind, but I'd rather help with the animals. I'm gonna be the third Dr. B. Langley when I grow up."

"It's good to have goals," Patrick remarked, impressed by the child's confidence.

"Mom says I'll prob'ly change my mind a dozen times before I go to college, but she knew she wanted to be a vet when she was my age, so I don't think I will."

"Some people do change their minds a dozen times—or more," Patrick said. "Look at me, for example. I went to college to get a business degree, but now I'm a rancher."

"So why didn't I see any cows when we drove in?" Brendan asked.

"Because they're in their winter pasture."

"What about other horses?"

"They're in the paddock behind the barn."

"Can I go see them?"

"Brendan, I told you not to bother Mr. Stafford," Brooke interjected before Patrick could respond.

"Mr. *Patrick*," her son reminded her.

"And he's not bothering me," Patrick said. "If I had somewhere else to be, I'd be there. Since I don't, I'm happy to take Brendan to see the other horses, if it's okay with you."

"It's okay with me." Then to Brendan, she said, "But remember the rules."

"I *always* remember the rules," he said, with an exaggerated eye roll.

"What are the rules?" Patrick asked, as they exited the barn and headed toward the paddock.

"Respect the animals and their space, do what she tells me when she tells me, and don't touch anything without permission."

"Those sound like reasonable rules," he said.

"Yeah," Brendan agreed. "But why does she have to remind me *Every. Single. Time?*"

"I'd guess it's because she wants to make sure you're safe," Patrick said. And though it really was just a guess, it made sense to him.

Apparently Brendan thought so, too, because he nodded.

Then he spotted the horses, and his big blue eyes suddenly got even bigger. "Wow. You sure do have a lot of horses."

"Twelve, including Ranger," he said. "But there are only nine out here now, because Levi and Dean—they're my ranch hands—each took a mount to ride out and check on the cattle."

When they reached the fence, the boy climbed up on the lowest rail and leaned his arms over the top. "What are their names?" he asked.

"The white one with the black spots is Pongo—"

"Like the dalmatian in the movie?"

"I don't know," Patrick admitted. "He already had his name when I got him, but I think that's a pretty good guess." Then he proceeded to point out and name the rest of the group. "The cream-colored one with the white mane and tail is Biscuit, the dark dappled gray is Stormy, the lighter gray is Cloudy, the pair of reddish bays with the black socks are Joe and Jackson, the paint—that's the brown one with big white splotches—is Picasso, the big black one is Midnight and her filly is Blue."

"Blue?" Brendan echoed quizzically.

Patrick shrugged. "Again, she had the name when I got her."

"So what is a dude ranch?" the boy asked.

"Where'd you hear that term?"

"My mom told my gramma that you're turning Mr. Sterling's property into a dude ranch."

"Actually, it's the Silver Star Vacation Ranch," he said.

"What's a vacation ranch?" Brendan asked.

"It's where people go to learn about and help with the daily operations of a ranch."

The boy's brow wrinkled. "That doesn't sound much like a vacation."

"Maybe not to you and me," he acknowledged. "But for those who live in crowded cities, it's an opportunity to escape the noise and traffic and experience a simpler lifestyle."

"I'd rather go to Disneyland," Brendan said.

Patrick chuckled at that. "I think I probably would, too, but other people like the idea of trail rides, fishing trips and cooking under the stars. And for younger guests, there will be riding lessons and other activities."

An admittedly vague description, but he hadn't yet figured out exactly what those other activities might be.

"You should also teach them how to take care of a horse," Brendan suggested. "Grandpa says it's important to repay a horse for letting you ride with proper care."

"That's a good point," Patrick said. "I'll add it to my list."

"Junior rodeo events are fun, too. At cowboy camp last summer, we learned how to rope a steer—well, it was actually a hay bale with fake horns," he admitted. "But it was still fun."

"What else did you do?"

"I won the ribbon for mutton busting," the boy said proudly. "And that was a real mutton."

"Maybe I should hire you as a junior consultant,"

Patrick mused, making a mental note to look into the cost of acquiring and caring for a couple of sheep.

"You mean like a job? That would be so cool!" Brendan said excitedly. "Would I get paid?"

"Maybe we should ask your mom what she thinks before we discuss those kinds of details."

"She'll think it's okay," the boy said confidently. "'Cause she knows you've got more money than brains."

Chapter Six

Please let the earth open up and swallow me now,
Brooke thought, as she heard the words come out of
her son's mouth.

Unfortunately, the universe didn't comply with her
request, forcing her to chastise him for repeating what
he'd obviously overheard of a private conversation.

"Brendan Langley, that was a completely inappro-
priate thing to say."

"But that's what you told Grandpa," Brendan said.

Because her son was nothing if not honest.

And still, the ground remained solid beneath her feet.

"I'm sure you must have misheard," she said.

"No, I didn't," Brendan insisted, shaking his head
for emphasis.

She slid a glance toward Patrick, trying to gauge

his reaction to Brendan's remark—or rather his repetition of her remark. The corners of the rancher's mouth twitched as he fought against a smile. Apparently he thought it was funny to watch her try to talk herself out of the corner she'd been boxed into.

"And even if you think that's what you heard," she continued to address her son, "you need to understand that some adult conversations aren't meant for your ears—or to be repeated."

"Does that mean I won't get paid?" Brendan directed this question to Patrick.

"Paid for what?" she asked, obviously having arrived on the scene after that part of the conversation.

"We can discuss that later," the rancher said. "How's Ranger?"

"It's only been a couple days," Brooke reminded him. "But at this point, there are no red flags."

"Coronet injuries are tricky," Brendan said solemnly. "If they don't heal prop'ly, they can cause perm'nent figurement or lameness."

"*Dis*figurement," Brooke corrected automatically.

"That's why I've chosen to pay someone with special expertise to care for Ranger rather than risk further damage," Patrick said to Brendan.

"That seems pretty smart to me," the boy decided, then turned to the horses again.

Brooke took a couple of steps back, away from the fence, and gestured with a jerk of her chin—a silent request for Patrick to follow.

"I owe you an apology," she said, when she was confident that they were out of earshot of her son. "And I am sorry."

"Sorry you said it or sorry your son repeated it?"

She just shook her head. "You're never going to let me forget this, are you?"

"I don't know… Never is a long time," he said. "And it's entirely possible that I do have more money than brains, but that's only because I'm unbelievably rich."

"And unbelievably humble," she remarked dryly.

He grinned. "But I was smart enough to get you to come back to my ranch."

"To take care of your horse."

"That was one reason," he acknowledged. "Another was that I really wanted another look at you."

She lifted a brow. "Are you flirting with me?"

"I'm trying," he admitted. "But flirting, not unlike sex, is an activity that's much more enjoyable with a partner."

"Well, I wish you luck finding one," she said.

"I'm looking at the one I want," he told her.

Her gaze skittered away.

"And I think you want me, too. That's why you brought your son with you today, to ensure there wouldn't be a repeat of what happened yesterday."

"What happened yesterday?" she asked, adopting a casual tone so that he wouldn't suspect how much she'd been affected by the kiss they'd shared.

But the slow curve of his lips warned that he wasn't fooled for a second. "Yesterday you plastered yourself against me and shoved your tongue down my throat."

"I did not," she denied hotly. "And it was *your* tongue that made first contact."

"Apparently you *do* remember what happened yesterday," he mused.

"It doesn't matter," she said. "Because what happened yesterday isn't going to happen again."

But it was a bold statement set on a shaky foundation, and they both knew it.

Sarah's Jeep pulled into the driveway as Brooke was buckling Brendan into his booster seat. Two minutes earlier, he'd wished he could talk the sexy vet into staying a while longer. Now he was glad she was on her way so that he wouldn't have to introduce the two women.

The older of his two sisters, Sarah had always had an uncanny ability to know when he was interested in a female, and she'd exploited that talent mercilessly over the years. No doubt she would only have to glance between Patrick and Brooke to know he was hot for the vet, and then she'd subject Brooke to a million questions.

"What are you doing here?" Patrick asked, when Sarah climbed out of her Jeep.

"It's good to see you, too, big brother," she said.

"I am happy to see you," he told her. "I'm just surprised because I thought you were in Vegas for the weekend."

"I got back this morning."

"And rushed over here because you missed me?"

"Because I heard that Ranger was hurt," his sister clarified.

"How could you possibly have heard that?" he wondered aloud. The only person he'd told about the horse's injury was his grandfather, in the hope that he would have been available to come out to take a look at the stallion. Unfortunately, one of Jesse Blake's own horses at Crooked Creek Ranch had been ready to foal for the first time and he hadn't been willing to leave her. Instead, he'd suggested that Patrick call Dr. Langley.

No doubt his grandfather had been referring to Bruce, but Patrick wasn't at all disappointed to find his beautiful daughter on his doorstep instead. "Gramps told Spencer, who of course told Kenzie, who asked me how the stallion was doing when I ran into her at The Daily Grind," Sarah said, explaining the source of her knowledge to him now. Spencer being their cousin and Kenzie his wife, who lived with their kids in the main house at Crooked Creek Ranch, where Gramps resided in the old bunkhouse.

"And you came right away to put your secret veterinarian skills to work?" Patrick teased his sister.

She punched him in the shoulder—playfully but not exactly lightly. "Maybe I did think I might be able to do something to help."

"There's not," he told her. "It's a coronary band injury that the vet has examined and treated."

"Is Ranger going to be okay?" she asked, sincerely concerned about the animal's welfare.

"Fingers crossed," he said. "But if you wanted to do something more…"

"Of course I do," she immediately replied.

"Great. You can make lunch."

Not surprisingly, his sister rolled her eyes at that suggestion. "You still haven't hired a cook?"

"I didn't see any point in hiring a cook before I had guests to feed."

"The point is that you'd have someone to make lunch for you rather than trying to manipulate your sister."

"That is a good point," he acknowledged. "But it seems kind of indulgent to have someone around to prepare meals only for me."

"It's not as if you can't afford it," she said.

"You'd think so, but most of my money has been invested in the property you're standing on."

Her eyes grew wide. "And you claim you're not a gambler."

"I know most of the family doesn't approve of what I'm doing here, but I thought you and Jenna would at least pretend to be supportive."

"You know we've always had your back," Sarah said.

And he did know it. As much as he'd always looked out for his sisters, they'd done the same for him. Gramps had dubbed them The Three Musketeers from an early age because they'd always had an "all for one and one for all" philosophy. Of course they'd had to rely on one another, as they'd often been left to their own devices while their parents spent most of their waking hours at Blake Mining, diligently adding to the family fortune.

Poor little rich kids.

"But having your back doesn't mean we don't worry about you," Sarah said to him now.

"You're worried because I chose to walk away from Blake Mining?" he guessed.

She shrugged. "You are a little young to be going through a midlife crisis."

"It's a simple career change, not a midlife crisis," he assured her.

"It's a big gamble," she said again.

"Speaking of which, how was Vegas?" he asked.

She let him get away with shifting the topic of conversation—at least for now.

"It was okay," she replied, with a half-hearted shrug.

"Did you lose all your money on the roulette wheel?"

"Blackjack," she told him.

"So what prompted this impulsive trip?" he asked.

"I didn't want to be stuck here, alone, on Valentine's Day," she admitted.

"Was it better to be alone in Vegas?" he asked. Then another thought occurred to him. "Or maybe you weren't alone—in which case, you can spare me the details."

"I wasn't alone," she said. "I went with a friend who was getting over a recent breakup and who decided that hooking up with a random guy was a better idea than hanging out with her also single friend."

"That sucks," he said.

She shrugged again. "It wasn't the worst Valentine's Day ever."

"I've never understood why there's so much focus put on a made-up holiday."

"If you think about it, all holidays are made up," she said.

"But only Valentine's Day was a conspiracy between the florists and candy makers who wanted an excuse to jack up the prices of their wares."

"So who did you buy flowers and chocolates for this year?" Sarah asked.

"No one." In fact, the date might have slipped right past without him even realizing it if he hadn't gone into town that night.

"Hmm… I thought you might have celebrated the occasion with Trinity, considering that she broke up with Christopher a few weeks back," Sarah said.

"We did have a drink at Diggers' Friday night."

"Which was Valentine's Day," she reminded him.

"Right."

"And after the drink?" she prompted.

"There was no 'after,' just a drink," he told her.

"Hmm…" she said again, somehow making the single syllable sound as if it was filled with meaning.

"So who is she?" Sarah pressed, when he didn't respond to her musing.

"Who is who?" he asked.

"The woman who inspired you to turn down a sure thing like Trinity?"

"Isn't it possible that I just wasn't in the mood for a hookup?" he countered.

"Possible," she allowed. "But not probable. I'm guessing it's the redhead who was getting into her truck as I drove up."

Yep, there were those uncanny instincts again.

"She must be someone special," Sarah continued. "Because you don't usually allow your…female companions… to hang around so late the next day."

"Brooke didn't spend the night," he said.

She nodded. "I should have realized. You're usually in a much better mood the morning after."

"Why are you here again?" he asked.

"I came to check on Ranger," she said. "And...I'm bored."

"You could get a job," he suggested.

"I have a job—Associate Director of Occupational Safety and Health at Blake Mining."

He snorted. "You have a paycheck."

"Yep," she agreed. "And one that I happily spend as fast as I earn it."

"Don't you want to actually do something with your life?" he asked, genuinely concerned that she was aimlessly going through the motions with little regard for her own happiness. Not unlike he'd done for far too long.

"Like what? Open a dude ranch?" Her skeptical tone left him in no doubt about what she thought of that idea.

"The Silver Star is a vacation ranch," he corrected automatically.

"Po-tay-to, po-tah-to," she said.

"And you know, maybe that's not such a bad idea," he decided.

"What?"

"You working here."

She waved her hands in front of her, clearly dismissing his suggestion. "Oh, no," she said. "You're *not* roping me into participating in this questionable venture."

"You're a people person, Sarah. You shouldn't be stuck in an office reading reports all day." Though his intention had been to turn the topic of conversation away from the sexy vet—and thank goodness Brendan had already been buckled into his booster seat, so his sister hadn't caught a glimpse of Brooke's son—his remark was nothing less than the truth. Sarah was good with people, sincere and empathetic, always willing to soothe and reassure others. Unlike Jenna, who liked to light the fuses and then sit back to watch the fireworks.

"We both know I'm only in my office a few hours a week," she said. "And you still haven't answered my question about your female visitor."

"Brooke is the vet who's been looking after Ranger's injury."

"What happened to Dr. Langley?"

"She's another Dr. Langley—his daughter, who works with him in his practice."

"This is all starting to make sense now," Sarah mused.

"What's starting to make sense?"

"When I saw Kenzie, I asked her about Buttercup's new foal, but apparently she hasn't had it yet, and Kenzie guessed it was going to be at least a few more days."

"And?" he prompted.

"Gramps has been a rancher his whole life. He's probably witnessed more livestock births than he can count."

"True," he acknowledged.

"So doesn't it seem a little strange that when you asked him to come out here to check on Ranger, he was too busy watching over an expectant mare who wasn't anywhere near ready to foal?"

"Obviously he misread the signs," he said, with a shrug.

"He didn't misread anything," Sarah denied. "He made an excuse about why he couldn't come out here so that you'd have to call the new vet."

Patrick couldn't imagine Jesse Blake going to such lengths in the vague hope of striking a romantic match for one of his grandchildren. "Our grandfather is hardly the type to play Cupid."

"I wouldn't have thought so, either," his sister agreed. "But he's had romance on his mind—and a definite spring in his step—since he's been dating Helen Powell."

He shuddered. "Aside from the fact that I don't want to think about Gramps and Helen, there's a major flaw in your theory."

"What's that?"

"There's no way Gramps could have known it would be Brooke who showed up instead of her dad."

"Sure there is. Gramps knows everyone in this town, and if he talked to someone who mentioned having a problem that required the vet, then he'd know the senior Dr. Langley would have been occupied and that another call to the clinic would result in his daughter coming out here," Sarah theorized.

The convoluted explanation left Patrick unconvinced.

But on the off chance that his sister was right, he'd have to talk to his grandfather about meddling in his personal life—and maybe say "thank you."

"I thought you might be waiting for Brendan to get home from school so you could bring him with you," Patrick remarked, when Brooke showed up at the Silver Star just before 4:00 p.m. the following day.

She shook her head. "I'd planned to be here around noon, but I got caught up at the Wallace farm, vaccinating the new kids." And then chatting with Howard

Wallace about his potential plans to expand his cheese offerings at the local farmers' market. As a result of that lengthy conversation, the vaccine cooler in the back of her truck now also contained samples of several new varieties that Howard had given her to try.

"I was riding fence with Levi and Dean and only got back a while ago myself, so I'm glad I didn't miss you," he said. "But if you ever do come by when I'm not around, feel free to do what you need to."

"I will," she assured him. "But I have no doubt you could handle Ranger's care yourself. It's not that complicated."

"But not my area of expertise, either," he told her.

"So what is your area of expertise?" she asked curiously.

"Market data analysis."

"A skill that will no doubt serve you well on trail rides and at cookouts," she remarked wryly.

"No doubt," he agreed with a grin.

When she'd finished with her task, instead of immediately packing up and heading out, she turned to him and said, "Can I ask you something?"

"As a matter of fact, I am free for dinner." He winked. "And breakfast."

"That's *not* what I wanted to know," she assured him.

"But still valuable information."

Though Brooke rolled her eyes, Patrick thought he saw a spark of amusement in their depths.

"Did you tell Brendan that you wanted him to be a consultant?" she asked him.

"Junior consultant," he clarified.

"Why?"

He shrugged. "It turns out he's got some pretty good ideas about the kinds of things kids might like to do when visiting a guest ranch, and since I didn't really have *any* ideas, it made sense. And I'm happy to pay for his time—unless you object to me spending time with your son?"

"You're not going to pay him," she said. "And I don't have any objections. I just want to be clear that spending time with Brendan isn't going to score any points with me."

"I'm not asking to spend time with him to score points with you," he said. "I happen to think he's a great kid."

"I didn't think you liked kids."

"I didn't think I did, either," he confided. "But it seems that I like Brendan. And I really like his mom."

"I'm flattered," she said. "But I'm not interested in having an affair, a fling or a one-night stand with you."

"I noticed you didn't dismiss the possibility of a relationship."

"I didn't think it was necessary, because everyone knows *you* don't do relationships."

"And *you've* been listening to gossip," he chided.

"So it's not true that you've never dated the same woman for more than three months?" she challenged.

He mentally reviewed his most recent romantic involvements. He'd dated Trinity for about five months altogether, but never for more than a few weeks at a time. Dana? No, that relationship hadn't lasted any more than six weeks. Kristie? About six weeks again. Shayla? Almost three months—until she'd asked him to accompany her to Flagstaff, Arizona, for Thanksgiving to meet the family. He'd taken a hard pass on that invitation.

Brooke was watching him, the hint of a smile tugging at the corners of her mouth.

He wanted to kiss the smile off her face. Or maybe he was just looking for an excuse to kiss her. Because after only one taste, he was addicted to her flavor, craving not just another sample but a feast.

But she was still waiting for a response to her question, so he finally said, "I dated Kimberly Ellis for almost two years."

"High school doesn't count," she told him.

He frowned, once again struck by the certainty that they'd both attended Westmount but unable to grasp any solid memory of her from back then. "How do you know that was high school?"

"Because I was in the same grade as Kimberly's sister, Emily."

Which meant that she would have been a freshman when he was a senior, and definitely not on his radar. "Okay, so I don't have a lot of experience with relationships," he conceded.

"Which is probably one of the few things we have in common," she said.

"You don't date a lot?"

"I've been on a total of three dates since Brendan was born and none at all in the past three years."

"Seriously?"

"I don't know why you sound surprised," she said. "The idea of dating a single mom sends most guys running in the opposite direction." She stared at him pointedly. "Or at least taking a big step back."

As he'd done, when she'd first told him that she had a child. But now that he'd spent some more time with her and met her son, the idea of dating a single mom didn't seem so scary. Instead, the prospect of spending more time with Brooke and Brendan was oddly appealing.

Chapter Seven

Over the next week, Brooke showed up at the ranch daily, if not on any particular schedule, squeezing in visits to the Silver Star around her other commitments. Sometimes she came on her own, and sometimes she brought Brendan with her. On the latter occasions, Patrick tried to make a point of spending some time consulting with his junior consultant.

Brendan really was a great kid, and Patrick had to give full credit to Brooke for raising a well-spoken and confident son on her own. Yeah, the boy was a little outspoken at times, but Patrick quite enjoyed their frank conversations.

Today after their consult, Brendan had asked if he could build a snow fort—a reminder to Patrick that the fresh fall of snow that had been a hassle for him to shovel off the walks that morning was a glorious world of opportunity for a child.

"Since you're here, I wondered if you might have time to check something else," Patrick said, as Brooke returned Ranger to his stall.

"What something else?" she asked.

He gestured to the animal that was curled up in the vacant stall across from Ranger's.

Brooke followed the direction he was pointing, her eyes widening when she spotted the curly-haired dog tucked in the corner. "You got a dog?"

"I didn't get anything," he denied. "It just suddenly appeared."

"When?"

"This morning—or maybe last night. But I didn't see it until this morning."

She cautiously stepped through the open gate. Watching her approach, the dog thumped its tail a few times, even as it ducked its head, as if anticipating a scolding—or maybe worse.

"I'm not going to hurt you," Brooke murmured softly. "I just want to see if you're wearing a collar."

But she paused a few feet away, respecting the animal's space, and lowered herself to her haunches. "Look at you, pretty girl," she said, in the same soothing tone. "Or are you a pretty boy?"

The dog rose to a crouched position and slowly crawled toward her.

"Pretty girl," Brooke decided. "She looks like a labradoodle to me."

She held herself still, letting the animal sniff her, and was rewarded with a swipe of tongue over her knuckles.

"Oh," she said softly, obviously already in love with the animal. She glanced up at Patrick as she stroked the fur beneath the dog's chin, making him wonder what he had to do to get the same kind of attention. "I'll bet she was abandoned and looking for a warm and dry place to sleep." She shook her head. "You wouldn't believe how many pets are dropped off by the side of a road or dumped in an empty field by people who have grown bored with them."

He frowned at that. "Why wouldn't they take them to a local shelter?"

"Because then they'd have to own up to their abandonment rather than pretend the animal just ran away," Brooke explained, as she continued to stroke and soothe the dog. "Although sometimes pets do escape through an open door or window and race off in search of adventure, then can't find their way home again."

"So someone might be looking for her?"

"It's possible. She doesn't have a collar, which means no tags, although she might be microchipped."

"How can you find that out?"

"I have a portable scanner in the truck," she said, giving the dog a last scratch behind the ears and rising to her feet.

She was back in only a few minutes, with the scanner in hand. She set it on the floor so the dog could sniff it and know there was no reason to be afraid.

"How do you know where to look?" Patrick asked, as she scanned the dog's back.

"Microchips are implanted just beneath the skin, right between the shoulder blades," she told him. "Although they can sometimes migrate to other places."

But she finished her check and shook her head as she set the scanner aside again.

"No microchip," he realized. "So what am I supposed to do with her now? Should I put up flyers saying 'Found Dog'?"

"You could," she said. "But if someone was looking for a lost pet, they probably would have called the clinic."

"How about flyers saying 'Dog Looking for a Good Home'?"

"Isn't this a good home?"

"I've got enough other animals to take care of without adding a dog to the mix," he said. Though this one really did seem to be a sweet-natured creature, and he'd often wished for a dog when he was younger.

"She wouldn't be much trouble," Brooke assured him. "Have you given her anything to eat?"

"I opened a can of stew," he admitted. "It was the only thing I could find that seemed suitable."

"Did she like it?"

"Gobbled it up like she was starving," he said. "Though she certainly doesn't look as if she is."

"You think she's overweight?" Brooke asked, a smile tugging at the corners of her mouth.

"You don't?"

"No," she said. "I think she's pregnant."

* * *

"I'm done with my fort!" Brendan announced as he entered the barn.

"Did you leave any snow on the ground?" Brooke asked, noting the amount of white stuff that covered her son.

He grinned, his white teeth a contrast to his red cheeks. "I made snow angels, too."

Then he spotted the dog.

"You got a dog?" he said, looking at Patrick with wide eyes.

"I think it might be more accurate to say that she got me," the rancher replied dryly.

Brendan dropped to his knees, far enough away so that the animal wouldn't feel threatened, and tugged off his snow-covered mittens. "What's his name?"

"Her," Brooke automatically corrected him.

"What's *her* name?" he asked.

"She doesn't have a name," Patrick said. "Or if she does, I don't know what it is."

"How come?"

"Because she's not my dog."

"She should have a name," Brendan said. "Maybe you could call her Chewie."

"Chewie?" Patrick echoed dubiously.

"Because she's furry, like Chewbacca," the boy explained.

"But she's a girl," Brooke said again.

Her son shrugged, clearly unconcerned about the gender implications of the suggested name, as the dog inched closer to the boy. When she was close enough, she nudged his arm with her nose, as if asking to be petted. He lifted his hand to oblige, and she licked his palm, making him giggle.

"Look, Mom. She likes me."

"Well, you are a pretty likable kid," she said.

Brendan flashed her a quick smile before shifting his attention back to the dog, stroking her gently.

"And Chewie's a good dog," he said. "Aren't you, Chewie?"

"How about Princess?" Brooke suggested as an alternative moniker.

"How about we stop trying to give the dog a name?" Patrick countered.

"Why are you afraid of naming her?" she asked.

"Because my grandfather always said that as soon as you name a stray, it becomes yours," he admitted.

"I'm pretty sure she's already yours," Brooke said.

"Princess is almost as good a name as Chewie," Brendan decided, siding with his mother. "If you think it's better for a girl dog."

Patrick's sigh was filled with resignation. "I don't care. You can call her whatever you want, because she's not going to be here very long."

"Want to bet?" Brooke challenged with a smile.

He shook his head. "I'm not keeping the dog and I'm definitely not keeping any puppies."

"She's gonna have *puppies*?" Brendan was clearly thrilled by the idea.

His mom nodded.

"When?" the little boy wanted to know.

"I'd guess in about four to five weeks," she said.

"Can you guess how many?" Patrick asked.

"Sure, I could guess," she told him. "But that's all it would be. If you want an accurate number, you could bring her into the clinic for an X-ray."

"If you aren't gonna keep the puppies, what'll happen to them?" Brendan asked, sounding worried.

"I'll find homes for them," Patrick promised.

"We could take one," her son offered helpfully.

"No, we can't," Brooke said firmly.

Brendan's face fell. "Why not?"

"Because puppies are a lot of work and I don't have the time or the patience to train one."

"I could help," he said.

"I'm sure you'd like to help," she acknowledged. "But who would look after a puppy all day when I'm at work and you're at school?"

"Maybe we could get *two* puppies," he suggested. "Then they could look after each other."

"A creative argument," Patrick said, sounding impressed by the boy's reasoning.

"But not a convincing one," she assured him, before turning to her son again. "Brendan, two puppies would be twice as much work—and twice as much money."

He pouted. "You never let me have anything I want."

She held his gaze for a minute, waiting for him to acknowledge the inaccuracy of his own words.

"You always say no when I ask for a puppy," he clarified.

"For the same reasons I just explained," she agreed.

"But I *really* want a puppy," Brendan told her.

"I know," she said. "But a puppy really wouldn't be

happy trapped inside our apartment for twenty hours every day."

"Your mom's right," Patrick chimed in, surprising Brooke by speaking out in support of her position. "A puppy needs a lot of attention and exercise and training."

She knew Brendan would have folded his arms over his chest if his hands hadn't been busy stroking the dog. Instead his lower lip poked forward to express his unhappiness that the adults were siding against him.

"Of course, the puppies are going to have to stay with their mom for several weeks after they're born," the rancher continued.

"At least six weeks," her son interjected.

Patrick nodded. "At least six weeks," he confirmed. "And during that time, if they're still here, you can visit them anytime you want."

"Anytime?" Brendan echoed hopefully.

"So long as it's okay with your mom," Patrick agreed.

A few days later, when Brooke returned to the Silver Star, she noticed a woman at the paddock fence, feeding treats to the horses. She had long dark hair and was wearing a fleece-lined denim jacket over faded jeans tucked into well-worn cowboy boots. Aware that she'd jumped to conclusions about Patrick's relationship with a female visitor to the ranch once before, Brooke cautioned herself against doing the same thing this time. But considering the rancher's reputation as a player, and the fact that he hadn't made another move on her since the kiss—aside from some casual flirting, which she suspected came as naturally to him as breathing—it wasn't unreasonable to conclude that he was seeing someone.

Brooke grabbed her backpack and the bag of puppy food she'd brought and headed toward the barn.

The brunette quickly moved away from the paddock and headed in the same direction. "Good morning," she said brightly.

Brooke echoed the greeting as the brunette hurried ahead to open the heavy barn door.

"Thanks."

"You must be the new vet," the other woman said, as she followed Brooke down the center aisle to Ranger's stall.

She dropped the bag of dog food just inside the enclosure where the canine had taken up residence, then nodded. "Brooke Langley."

"I'm Sarah," the brunette said.

"It's nice to meet you," Brooke said, as she turned her attention to the stallion. Well accustomed to the routine by now, Ranger patiently complied with her directions as she tied him.

Sarah watched Brooke as she worked. "I feel so guilty that I was out of town when he was injured," she said. "I've been helping Patrick exercise the horses and I can't help but wonder if Ranger escaped the paddock because he needed a good run."

"You spend a lot of time here, then?" Brooke asked, her curiosity piqued by the woman's revelation.

"It's a good excuse to get away from Miners' Pass."

She recognized the most exclusive address in town,

where she knew Patrick's family lived in one of the biggest of the big houses on the street. "Did you grow up near Mr. Stafford?" she asked, deliberately using the rancher's formal title.

"Too close for comfort sometimes," Sarah said wryly.

The girl next door, Brooke guessed.

"He was a complete pain in my ass growing up, and yet I can't help but miss him now that he's gone," she confided. "But I guess most little sisters probably feel that way about their big brothers."

"So you're Patrick's other sister," Brooke realized, as she began wrapping Ranger's hoof again.

"Have you already met Jenna?"

"Not formally, but our paths kind of crossed," she said.

"And since I look nothing like Jenna, you probably thought I was one of Patrick's legions of female admirers," Sarah guessed, sounding amused.

"The possibility crossed my mind."

"He does have a reputation," his sister acknowledged. "Though the trail of broken hearts isn't quite as long or wide as the rumor mill would lead you to believe. In fact, I wouldn't say the hearts were even broken—more likely just a little bit dented.

"Because for all his faults, and I know he has them, Patrick is unflinchingly honest with the women he goes out with to prevent anyone getting hurt. Those who do are the ones who refuse to believe him when he says he isn't looking for any kind of long-term relationship."

"How admirable," Brooke remarked dryly, at the same time wondering if Patrick's sister was trying to send her a message. Of course, the rancher had already relayed that message himself—loud and clear.

Sarah chuckled. "I can see why my brother likes you."

Before she could figure out an appropriate response to that, she heard the barn door opening again, followed by the sound of boots on concrete before Patrick appeared.

"Are you still here?" he asked.

"I'm just finishing up," Brooke told him.

The rancher shook his head. "I wasn't talking to you."

"Apparently I'm the one who's worn out my welcome," Sarah remarked.

"I didn't say that," her brother disagreed. "But when you left the house, almost an hour ago, you told me that you were leaving."

"And I am." Sarah touched her lips to Patrick's cheek, then waved in the vet's direction. "It was nice to meet you, Brooke."

"You, too, Sarah."

"If I'd realized she was still here, I would have come out to rescue you sooner," Patrick said to Brooke, when Ranger had been returned to his stall.

"Did I look like I needed rescuing?"

"No," he admitted. "But Sarah can be nosy at times, especially when she's prying for details about a woman in my life."

"I'm not in your life," she pointed out. "Just on the periphery."

"For now," he said, with a grin that sent a jolt of awareness through her body.

"I brought a bag of special puppy food for Princess," she said. "It will ensure she gets the energy and calcium she needs."

"That was a subtle shift in the conversation," he teased.

Brooke shrugged. "I don't have time for subtlety. I've got a bearded dragon with a possible respiratory infection waiting for me at the clinic."

"You treat lizards?"

"They aren't my specialty, but I'll check it out and refer it to a reptile vet, if necessary."

"Fair enough. But one of these days, when you've got some time, we'll get back to this conversation—and other unfinished business."

It was easy enough to disregard his words, but the intensity of his gaze reminded Brooke of the single kiss they'd shared—and tempted her with the promise of so much more.

Brooke Langley and Lori Banner became best friends in third grade when they realized they shared the same initials in reverse order. They stayed best friends through elementary and high schools before going away to different colleges. Now that Lori worked in the radiology department at Memorial Hospital in San Diego, the friends didn't get to see one another very often, but they did FaceTime once a month and texted whenever there was news to share, or just because.

So when Lori had reached out to say that she was

going to be in town for the weekend, of course Brooke was eager to see her, and they made plans to meet at Diggers' for dinner Saturday night.

"Are you goin' on a date?" Brendan asked, as he watched his mom brush mascara onto her lashes in preparation for a rare girls' night out.

Brooke chuckled at that. "No, honey. I'm having dinner with Aunt Lori tonight."

"Oh," he said, sounding disappointed. "Why don't you ever go on dates?"

She slid the wand back into the tube and twisted it closed.

"Because I've already got a number one guy," she said, playfully ruffling his hair.

"But it'd be kinda cool if you had a boyfriend," he said. "'Cause then you could get married and he'd be my dad."

Aching for her little boy, she turned away from the mirror to give her full attention to him.

"A few dates doesn't necessarily lead to marriage," she cautioned.

"I know," he said. "But you've gotta start somewhere, right?"

"And I know you'd really like a dad," she said. "But you've got an awesome grandpa who's taking you go-karting at Adventure Village tonight."

"Grandpa's the best, but a grandpa's not the same as a dad."

"No, he's not," she agreed.

"So I'm just sayin', I wouldn't mind if you wanted

to go out on dates sometimes," he continued, clearly unwilling to let the subject drop.

"I'll keep that in mind," she promised. "But right now I need to finish getting ready so I'm not late meeting Aunt Lori, okay?"

"Okay," he said.

Half an hour later, after she'd left Brendan with her parents, she was walking toward Diggers' when she saw her friend approaching from the other direction.

"Good timing," they said in unison. Then they both laughed.

After sharing a quick hug, they entered the restaurant, already chatting away as if it had only been days rather than weeks since they were last together.

"I'm so glad you were available tonight," Lori said when they were waiting for their meals.

"I would have canceled any other plans to make myself available," Brooke assured her, although they both knew that the chances of her having plans more elaborate than a bowl of popcorn and a movie with her son were slim to none. "Now tell me what inspired this impulsive trip home."

"I met someone," her friend blurted out, obviously unable to contain the happy news a moment longer.

"Someone from Haven?" Brooke guessed.

Lori shook her head. "No, he lives in California."

"Then why are you here instead of there?"

"Because, as you know, I have a habit of jumping into relationships with both feet and I'm determined to take things slow this time."

"In other words, the only way you could be sure

you wouldn't jump his bones was to leave the state," Brooke teased.

"Something like that," Lori agreed. "And he's a firefighter, with fabulous muscles in addition to great bones, so I think I deserve some credit for holding out this long."

"How long is this long?" she asked.

"I met him three weeks ago," her friend said.

"So why am I only hearing about him now?" Brooke wondered. But she didn't give Lori a chance to answer before continuing, "What's his name? Where did you meet him? What did you do on your first date?"

Her friend was more than willing to share all the details during dinner. Of course, she was interrupted on several occasions by other diners stopping by the table just to say hello or to ask Lori about California or to describe a pet's ailment and request a diagnosis from Dr. Langley—who always suggested they make an appointment because there was no way for her to know what was wrong without examining the animal in question.

But when Lori had finally revealed everything that she knew about hottie firefighter Matthew, it was evident that she was well on her way to falling in love, and Brooke was sincerely happy for her friend.

"It's time for you to get out there, too," Lori said, her tone gentle but firm.

"Have you been talking to my son?"

"Not yet, but I'm not going back to San Diego until I get my fill of Brendan cuddles," her friend promised. "Why?"

"He seemed disappointed that I wasn't going on a date tonight," she confided.

"Obviously your son understands that his mom is an incredible woman who deserves to share her life with an equally incredible man."

Brooke snorted at that. "I think Brendan just wants a dad."

"Well, of course the incredible man would also be a fabulous father," Lori said.

"Of course," she agreed.

"I know you're skeptical," her friend said. "But I promise—one day you're going to meet a man who'll make you forget all about that idiot who contributed to Brendan's DNA."

As an image of Patrick Stafford materialized in her mind, Brooke realized she might already have met that man.

Unfortunately, the sexy rancher had no interest in being anyone's father.

And by the end of the second week, Brooke had stopped worrying—or secretly hoping—that Patrick might make another move. Because the fact was, since the day of that first kiss, they were rarely ever alone together. Frequent visitors to the Silver Star included each of his sisters, various cousins and friends, and on one occasion, she'd even crossed paths with his grandfather. But Brooke never saw, or even heard mention of, his parents visiting.

What she did hear, from his sister Jenna, was that Liz and Derrick Stafford were far too busy to take an interest in their son's "little ranch" and that they were certain he'd be back behind a desk at Blake Mining before the end of the summer. Of course his relationship with his parents was none of her business, but she couldn't help but feel sorry that he couldn't count on their support as he embarked on a new venture—and even more grateful to know that she'd always had the support of her own.

Chapter Eight

On Saturday, Brendan was with his mom at the Silver Star when she got a message from the clinic's after-hours answering service that a local sheep farmer was frantic over the possibility that the new rams he'd introduced to his flock might be infected with a fatal degenerative disease. After Brooke had finished with Ranger, she called the farmer back, asked a few pointed questions about the origins of the suspect animals and their behavior, and agreed that the flock should be quarantined and tested—neither a quick nor easy job.

Tucking her phone back into her pocket, she exited the barn in search of her son. Brendan had gone outside to play fetch with Princess, promising to be careful not to throw too far so the pregnant dog didn't overexert herself.

"Come on, Brendan. We have to go."

"But we just got here," he protested.

"I've got an emergency situation to deal with," she said, knowing the information wouldn't make her son any happier but would compel him to move.

"What? Where?" he asked, already on his feet and handing Princess's slobbery ball to the rancher.

"Just down the road," she said. "But I have to take you to Gramma's first."

"Why can't I go with you?" Brendan asked.

At the same time Patrick said, "Why can't he stay here?"

"Yeah." Brendan immediately latched on to that option. "Why can't I stay here?"

"Because I don't know how long I'm going to be," she responded to both of them.

"I'm sure I can keep him entertained until you get back," Patrick said.

"It could be a couple hours," Brooke warned.

"And the sooner you leave, the sooner you'll get back," he pointed out.

It would certainly be convenient not to have to drive all the way into town and back again. But still she hesitated, suspecting that the rancher didn't have a clue what he was getting himself into. "Are you sure?"

"I'm sure." Patrick put his hands on her shoulders and turned her toward her truck. "Go."

"Okay," she said. "Brendan, I'm going."

He tipped his head back and puckered his lips for a quick kiss, then raced back to Princess.

Patrick puckered his lips, too, the twinkle in his eye challenging her.

Never one to back down from a challenge, Brooke gave him the same perfunctory peck that she'd given to her son.

So why did it feel completely different?

Even several hours later, Patrick didn't regret offering to let Brendan stay at the ranch while Brooke rushed off to deal with the emergency that had called her away. The boy was smart and curious and fun, but he was also a kid without a dad, and Patrick knew he wasn't the right man to step into that role.

Brendan had shared enough details about his day-to-day activities to reveal that his grandparents were very involved in his life. But Brooke's son had never mentioned a father, and it seemed that no one knew anything about the man who'd apparently never set foot in Haven and had no contact with the kid.

His choice? Patrick wondered. Or hers?

If he'd fathered a child—and thank God (or maybe only the diligent and proper use of birth control) that had *not* happened—he wouldn't have walked away from his responsibilities. He might not have been thrilled by the news of an unplanned pregnancy, but he would have done the right thing.

And he sure as hell wouldn't have let anyone keep him away from his child.

So what was the story with Brendan's father? And why did it even matter to Patrick if his only interest was in Brendan's mother?

He was puzzling over that question when Brendan asked, completely out of the blue, "Do you have a girlfriend?"

"Not right now I don't," he said.

"Why not?"

"Oh, um…because I've been busy working to get the ranch ready and haven't really had the time for a relationship."

"My mom's pretty busy, too," the boy confided. "Maybe that's why she doesn't have a boyfriend."

"Maybe," Patrick agreed.

"She says that she doesn't need any man in her life but me, but I'm prob'ly not gonna live with her forever, and then she'll be alone."

"Well, I'm sure she has a few years before she has to worry about an empty nest," he said, trying to lift some of the heavy concern he could see weighing on the boy's slender shoulders.

"But she's never had a boyfriend."

Patrick felt as if he should caution the boy against sharing family confidences with outsiders, but it was obvious Brendan didn't think of him as an outsider, and that made him feel surprisingly good.

"If you wanted a girlfriend, maybe you could talk my mom into being your girlfriend," Brendan suggested now.

"It doesn't really work like that," he said. "A boy and girl both have to want to be together. It's not something they can be talked into."

"But you like my mom, don't you?" he asked, sounding almost desperately hopeful.

"Yes, I like your mom," he confirmed. A whole lot more than he probably should, considering the complicated circumstances of their respective lives.

"And she likes you," Brendan said. "I know she does 'cause she puts that shiny stuff on her lips before we come over here."

"Does she?" he asked, both surprised and pleased by this revelation.

The boy nodded. "And she doesn't do it when we're going to the Rolling Meadows or the Circle G."

"Really?" he mused.

Brendan nodded. Then his brow furrowed as a new thought occurred to him. "Is it me? Am I the reason you don't want to date my mom?"

"What? No," Patrick denied. Because while he'd never before wanted to get involved with a woman tangled up with child-size responsibilities, he couldn't seem to resist Brooke.

And as it turned out, her kid was pretty irresistible, too.

"Where would you get an idea like that?" he asked now.

"My friend Mason said his mom's boyfriend dumped her because he didn't want to be a dad to someone else's kid."

"Then I'd say Mason's mom is better off without him."

"That's what she said," Brendan told him.

"Well, she's right," Patrick said, hating to think that any child would ever feel responsible because a man was selfishly unwilling to step up. As he'd been unwilling to do. But now that he'd had a chance to get to know both Brooke and Brendan a little bit better, he was starting to reconsider his position.

"So what do you think about dating my mom?" the boy pressed, clearly unwilling to give up on the idea.

"I think your mom doesn't need you to play matchmaker," Patrick said gently. "She's a smart, beautiful and amazing woman who wouldn't have any trouble finding someone to go out with if she was interested in dating."

Brendan rolled his eyes. "But I want her to go out with someone I like hanging out with, too."

"You know, you and I can hang out even if I'm not dating your mom," he pointed out.

"Maybe," Brendan said dubiously. "Until she starts dating someone else."

Yeah, Patrick silently agreed. *That would really suck.*

"I'm so sorry," Brooke said, when Patrick opened the door in response to her knock a short while later.

"You can stop apologizing anytime now," he told her, a reference to the multiple text messages she'd sent throughout the afternoon doing just that.

"No, I can't, because I know when you offered to let Brendan hang out, you thought it would only be for an hour or so, and I've been gone—" she glanced at her watch and winced "—more than five hours."

And he could tell, by the weariness in her eyes and the slump of her shoulders, that she'd been working hard for all of those hours.

She sniffed the air. "And it's obviously dinnertime

because you're cooking." She tilted her head, giving him a closer study. "You cook?"

He ignored her question to ask his own. "Are you hungry?"

Her stomach growled an immediate response.

He chuckled.

"Lunch was a long time ago," she confided.

"Then come on in and wash up for dinner," he said.

"Oh, no," she protested. "I wasn't fishing for an invitation."

"I know, but I've been holding dinner for you."

"You cooked for me?" she asked, clearly taken aback by that possibility even more than the fact that he could cook.

"I cooked because I was hungry," he clarified. "I cooked enough so that you and Brendan could eat, too."

"Where is Brendan?"

"Watching TV in the family room. He's already eaten," Patrick told her.

"He has?"

He nodded. "Your son was adamant that six o'clock is dinnertime, so I made sure he had his dinner at six o'clock."

"He gets that from my dad—a definite creature of habit," she acknowledged, making her way to the sink to wash up.

"What can I get you to drink?" he asked. "Beer? Wine?"

"A big glass of water, please," she said, because she was parched. "And maybe half a glass of wine?" Because after the day she'd had, she deserved a little indulgence.

"I've got a Napa Valley merlot or a Finger Lakes pinot noir," he said, as he filled a tall glass with water from the dispenser in the door of the fridge.

"Your choice," she said.

He gave her the water, then uncorked the pinot noir and poured it into two glasses, passing one to Brooke.

"Thank you," she said. "For everything today."

"Not a problem." He opened the oven to retrieve the two plates he'd left warming.

Brooke lifted herself onto one of the stools as he set the plates on the island.

"Dig in," he urged, taking a seat beside her and picking up his own fork.

Brooke didn't need to be told twice.

"Mmm," she said, after chewing and swallowing her third mouthful. "This is really good."

"It's not fancy but it's filling," he agreed.

"My mom makes a good meat loaf," she said. "But I'm not sure it's as good as this."

"Brendan seemed to think mine was better than Gramma's," he told her.

She chuckled. "He'll tell her that, too."

"I get the impression that he spends a lot of time with his grandparents."

"Probably more with them than with me," she confided. "I'm sure it was a nice change of pace for him to spend the day with someone different."

"Does Brendan ever see his dad?" he asked, his tone casual.

She stiffened in response to the question and glanced toward the wide entranceway that led to the family room, as if to ensure that her son was still engrossed in his television program and not within earshot. "Didn't we have this conversation already?"

"We didn't have a conversation. You said Brendan didn't have a father and that was the end of it."

"And nothing has changed since then," she told him.

"You didn't get pregnant by yourself," Patrick pointed out.

"No," she acknowledged. "But that's where his involvement ended."

She set her fork and knife on top of her empty plate. "Thank you for dinner," she said, clearly indicating that she'd said everything she intended to say on the subject of Brendan's father.

And once again, it wasn't much at all.

Unwilling to push and risk her further withdrawal, he said, "I figured you'd be happy to have a hot meal at the end of a long day."

"Truthfully, I would have been happy with a peanut butter sandwich," she said, pushing away from the island to carry her plate and glass to the sink. He followed with his own. "A hot meal pushes me beyond happy all the way to ecstatic."

He chuckled at that as he set his dishes down and drew her into his arms.

"Patrick," she said, sounding wary.

"Brooke," he echoed, amused.

"Ecstatic doesn't mean easy," she told him.

"You mean you're not going to let me have my way

with you while your son is watching *SpongeBob* on TV?" he asked, with feigned disappointment.

She smiled then. "Not this time."

"And now you've given me hope that there's going to be a next time," he warned.

"I didn't mean to," she said. "I'm not trying to string you along."

"I know," he assured her. "I just thought that maybe it was time to finally finish that conversation we started a long time ago."

"I've had a really long day. And so have you," she said.

"Okay, we'll skip the conversation," he decided and lowered his mouth to hers.

It was a casual kiss—teasing, testing—and Brooke knew that if she pulled away, he'd let her go.

She didn't pull away.

Though she still had concerns about acting on the attraction between them, she couldn't object to a kiss.

Sensing her acquiescence, one of his hands settled on her hip while the other slid up her spine to cup the back of her head as he deepened the kiss. She opened for him, not just willing but eager to meet the searching thrust of his tongue with her own.

Did he draw her closer?

Or did she lean into him?

She didn't know. She only knew that suddenly her breasts were pressed against his hard chest, and electricity was sparking through her veins, igniting a deeper desire.

She clung to him, her fingers digging into the soft

flannel that covered his broad shoulders, and briefly fantasized about tearing the fabric open to expose his bare skin, to examine and explore the taut muscles with her hands, with her mouth. To touch and taste him all over.

She was shocked by the explicitness of her own fantasy, and the desire that pulsed through her. A desire that she couldn't give in to. Not here. Not now. Not with this man.

Because Patrick Stafford wasn't just handsome and charming. The way she felt when she was with him was far too reminiscent of the way she'd felt when she was with Xander. And she'd promised herself, long ago, that she would learn from her mistakes.

She eased her lips away from his and drew in a long breath, filling her lungs with air.

"That was definitely a sweet end to the meal," he said. "And dangerously addictive."

He was right on both counts, and the truth only made her more wary. "What are we doing here, Patrick?"

"I thought we were enjoying spending time together," he said.

Which sounded simple and easy, and yet… "I don't want to get used to this."

"Because you don't trust me to stick?" he guessed.

"Because you don't want to stick," she reminded him. "You want to have some fun and move on, and that's fine for you, but I can't do that."

"How do you know without giving it a try?"

She started to dismiss his suggestion out of hand, then realized there might be some merit to it. She was afraid of giving in to the feelings he stirred inside her because she was afraid of getting hurt again.

But what if she could keep things light and casual? What if she could just enjoy being with him?

It was a tantalizing possibility.

"I don't know that I'm capable of having a casual relationship without the expectation of something more," she said. "But I'm sure that Brendan isn't."

"I'm not following."

"He's a seven-year-old boy without a father, and he's already getting attached to you," she explained.

"We're buddies," he said.

"And that's great," she agreed. "Until he starts looking at you as something more than a buddy."

Patrick immediately shook his head. "He's too smart for that."

"You'd think so," she said, as the theme song of her son's favorite cartoon alerted her to the show's conclusion. "But that's not a chance I'm willing to take."

She wasn't surprised that Brendan fell asleep in the truck on the drive home. She *was* surprised that he didn't conk out until they were less than five minutes from their destination. Prior to that, he'd kept himself awake by excitedly recounting every minute of his day with Mr. Patrick.

While she'd been testing potentially infected sheep, she'd barely had a moment to think about her son, but when she did, she'd worried that he might be bored or pestering Patrick with 1001 questions. Based on Brendan's retelling of the day's events, he definitely had *not* suffered from boredom.

In fact, it sounded as if he'd really enjoyed the time he'd spent at the Silver Star. His busy day at the ranch had included a horseback ride (*with a helmet*, he was quick to assure her), helping to groom and feed the horses, "consulting" with Mr. Patrick on his proposed child-friendly ranch activities, playing board games—which usually ranked significantly lower than video games in his estimation but had apparently been a lot of fun with Mr. Patrick—and finally, after dinner, some quiet time in front of the television.

Considering the amount of fresh air and exercise he'd got, it was no wonder exhaustion had finally caught up with him. But not before he'd commented, in a casual tone, that it had almost been like having a dad. The offhand remark confirming that Brooke was right to be worried about her son's growing attachment to the rancher.

Another worry was that, by the time she pulled into her driveway, the earlier threat of snow had turned into the real thing. She suspected the forecasted four to six inches would be blanketing the ground by morning, and though it was just a light dusting right now, she parked in the garage to save herself having to clear snow off her truck later.

Though Brendan was growing fast and getting heavy, she didn't like to wake him just so he could walk upstairs to his bed. Instead, she unbuckled his seat belt and lifted him into her arms, all too aware that her days of being able to carry her not-so-little-anymore boy were already numbered.

She pulled back his covers and lowered him onto the bed, then gently stripped him out of his coat, removed his hat and boots, and pulled the covers up again.

Of course, he hadn't brushed his teeth, but she knew that if she woke him now to perform the task, he'd be wide-awake until the wee hours of the morning—and so would she. So she only touched her lips to his forehead and left him sleeping.

He was the love of her life, but recently she'd started to realize that being a mother wasn't the whole of her identity. Her growing and deepening feelings for Patrick reminded her that she was also a woman, with a woman's wants and needs. And while she had no doubt that the rancher would be able to satisfy her desires, she knew that falling for a man like Patrick Stafford could only end in heartache.

But it was Brendan's tender heart that she worried about even more than her own. After only two weeks, it was obvious that her son had become attached to the rancher. He asked about him every day and was always disappointed to learn that Brooke had gone to the Silver Star without him.

Obviously it had been foolish to believe that the strong and steady presence of Brendan's grandfather could somehow make up for the absence of a father in his life.

But it would be a mistake to count on Patrick Stafford to fill that void for more than a few hours.

* * *

Melissa Stafford didn't believe in signs.

In her opinion, those who waited for signs wasted an awful lot of time waiting, while those who truly wanted something went after it.

So she didn't think it was a sign when she received a text message from her cousin Patrick in Haven only a few hours after she'd been wishing she had somewhere to go to get away from Seattle. But she did recognize it as an opportunity.

"Are you sautéing or snoozing, Stafford?"

She ignored the snarky question and tipped the pan so the browned cremini mushrooms spilled over the freshly grilled striploin plated beside a handful of roasted baby potatoes and a trio of asparagus spears.

"I'm taking a break," she called out, confident that her vacant station would quickly be filled by one of the eager apprentices who hovered around the kitchen at Alessandro's, desperate for the opportunity to do something.

She pulled her phone out of her pocket and reread Patrick's message as she slipped out the back door.

"I thought you'd be working on a Saturday night," he said, when he connected the call.

"You caught me on my smoke break."

She heard the frown in his voice when he asked, "Since when do you smoke?"

"I don't," she admitted. "But the smokers get to skip out of the kitchen for ten minutes every few hours, so I've started carrying a pack of cigarettes in my pocket."

"Is your boss really that much of a tyrant?"

"You have no idea. Anyway, your message said you're looking to hire a cook—is this for your dude ranch?"

"You know about that?"

"Are you kidding?" she asked. "The whole family's taking bets on how long you're going to stick it out."

"Nice to know everyone has such faith in my abilities," he remarked dryly.

"It's not your abilities they doubt but your commitment," she told him. "My dad says you've had five different positions at Blake Mining in the past five years."

"Six years," he said, as if that made a difference. "But I'm going to make this work."

"I believe you," Melissa said. Truthfully, she'd always thought the reason he bounced around from job to job at Blake Mining was that he was never happy there. And while she didn't know if this current venture would make him any happier, she had her own reasons for throwing her support behind him.

"I appreciate your vote of confidence," Patrick said.

"And to show how much I believe in you, I'll take the job."

There was a pause as he took a moment to process her unexpected offer.

"You want to leave your fancy restaurant in Seattle to cook for guests at my vacation ranch in Haven?"

"I do," she confirmed.

"Why?" he asked, sounding just a little bit wary.

"I need a change of scenery," she replied, aiming for a tone that was casual and carefree and not at all desperate.

"Not a lot of people come to northern Nevada for the scenery," he pointed out.

"This is a once-in-a-lifetime opportunity," she told him. "If you were smart, you'd grab hold of it with both hands before I change my mind."

Or started to beg, which would undoubtedly set off all kinds of alarm bells in her cousin's mind.

"What's it going to cost me?" he asked.

"Whatever you had budgeted for a cook's salary, plus a room for me on-site," she impulsively decided, because the salary wasn't nearly as important as the opportunity to get out of Seattle.

"I can manage that."

"Then I'll give my two weeks' notice after the restaurant closes tonight," she said, grateful that she could see not just a road out of her dead-end life but possibilities for a new start in Haven.

Chapter Nine

Brooke was awakened early Sunday morning by fifty-five pounds of jubilant child jumping on her bed.

"Wake up, Mom!"

She pulled the covers up over her head. "It's Sunday," she reminded her son. "The one day of the week that I get to sleep in."

"But it snowed last night and I wanna go tobogganing."

She opened one eye and peeked out from under the covers. "It's not even eight o'clock."

Then her cell phone chimed, and she sighed wearily as she reached for it to check the message.

"Apparently Grandpa's awake, too," she noted. "He says you've got half an hour to get ready or he's going tobogganing without you."

"Yikes! I've gotta get dressed."

"And eat some breakfast," Brooke said, pushing back the covers. "You can't tackle snow-covered hills on an empty stomach."

Of course, Brendan was already gone, racing back to his room in search of something to wear.

She wrapped herself in a plush robe, stuffed her feet into fuzzy slippers and headed to the kitchen to pop some frozen waffles into the toaster. While she was waiting for the pastries to heat, she sent a quick reply to her dad.

He'll be ready. Thank you so much! You've totally made his day. xo

Just then, she heard her son's footsteps coming down the hall. "I'm ready!" Brendan announced, sliding across the tiles in his sock feet.

She gave him a quick once-over. "Do you have a T-shirt on under that hoodie?"

"No, but—"

She lifted an arm and pointed to his bedroom.

He sighed but went to do her bidding.

When he came back again, his breakfast was ready: the OJ poured into his favorite cup and toasted waffles cut into strips to be dunked in the little container of syrup.

While he was eating, she made herself a cup of coffee, using the last pod in the cupboard. She added *coffee* to the grocery list on the fridge, beneath *likrish* and *mashmelos*—obviously her son's additions and proof that he was much better at math than spelling.

She'd just taken a first sip when Brendan pushed away from the island, setting his cup on top of the plate and carefully carrying both to the sink.

"Thanks, Mom." He returned to press sticky lips to her cheek.

"You're welcome," she said. "Now brush your teeth, and make sure you clean every tooth because you didn't brush last night."

"Okay," he agreed.

She finished her coffee while he was occupied with that task, then helped him wriggle into his snow pants and ski jacket. By the time his grandfather knocked on the door, Brendan was ready.

"How is it that you have so much more energy than I do?" Brooke asked her dad.

He grinned. "I don't have to be up with a seven-year-old every morning—and I love tobogganing."

She knew it was true. She had so many memories of racing down the snow-covered hills with her brothers and her dad, then returning home to warm numb hands around steaming mugs of hot chocolate.

"Well, then, be safe and have fun," she said.

"We will," he promised. Then he winked at his grandson. "And we'll let Gramma know when we're on our way back, so she can have the hot chocolate ready, right?"

"Right!" Brendan confirmed with enthusiasm.

Brooke was smiling as they drove away, but she was going to need another cup of coffee to get through a day that had started far too early. Of course, that required getting dressed and heading over to The Daily Grind, where she could grab a doughnut or muffin to go with her coffee. And since she knew her mom was alone this morning, she opted for two of the vanilla lattes Sandra enjoyed—on the rare occasions that she let herself indulge—and two maple pecan Danishes.

"You were late getting home last night," Sandra remarked, when Brooke stopped by with her offerings from the local coffee shop.

She didn't bother to ask how her mother knew. No doubt she hadn't gone to sleep until she'd seen her daughter's vehicle pull into the driveway. Now that Brooke was a parent herself, she understood why her mom had never been able to sleep until she knew her children were safe in their own beds.

"Brendan stayed at the Silver Star when I got called out to Rolling Meadows, and when I got back, Patrick invited me to stay for dinner."

Sandra broke off the corner of her Danish. "What did he make?"

"Meat loaf with mashed potatoes and green beans."

"Was it good?"

"Very good," Brooke admitted.

"A man who can cook… Imagine that," her mother mused.

"Dad can cook."

"Breakfast," Sandra said. "If he ever tackled something like meat loaf, I'd fall off my chair. Then I'd fall head over heels in love—if I wasn't already there."

Brooke rolled her eyes. "Well, my heart is holding

out for something that will hopefully last a little longer than an evening meal."

"But you like Patrick," her mom noted.

"I like him," she admitted.

"Why does that sound like a reluctant admission?"

"Because he's Patrick Stafford."

"And?" Sandra prompted.

"We went to the same high school," she reminded her mother. "And even though he graduated when I finished my freshman year, his reputation lived on."

"Everyone has a past," Sandra noted. "Why are you holding Patrick's against him?"

"Because I don't think he's changed."

"He's been good for Brendan," her mom pointed out. "Since the first time you took him out to the Silver Star, your son hasn't stopped talking about 'Mr. Patrick.'"

"I know." Brooke sighed.

"Or maybe that's the real problem," Sandra suggested.

"I never thought he was missing out, not having a father, because he's got the world's greatest grandfather," she confided.

"But it's not the same thing as having a father," her mom noted. "So maybe it's good for Brendan to spend time with Patrick."

"And maybe it's a shortcut to heartbreak," Brooke said. "Don't forget the way Patrick reacted when I first told him that I had a child."

"It's not unusual for a man to think he isn't ready to be a father—until he is," Sandra remarked. "Anyway, actions speak louder than words, and Patrick has been there for you. *And* for Brendan."

"Maybe he's enjoying the novelty of hanging out with a kid," she allowed. "But when the responsibilities get too real, he's likely to back off again."

"Do you really think so?"

She sighed. "I don't know what to think. And I don't like not knowing what to think, how to feel."

"You've got to stop punishing yourself for falling in love with the wrong man," her mom said gently.

"I'm not," she denied.

"Aren't you?"

"I stopped loving Xander a long time ago."

"So why haven't you let yourself love anyone else?" Sandra asked.

"My life doesn't exactly lend itself to romantic relationships," Brooke reminded her. "Being a single mom with a busy job doesn't leave a lot of time for anything else."

"And yet you've managed to find time to spend with Patrick."

"At the Silver Star, where I treat his injured horse."

"And when Ranger's injury is healed?" her mother asked.

"We'll find out soon enough," Brooke said. "Because I suspect he'll be ready to return to his herd by the end of next week."

"It's healing nicely," Jesse Blake said, with an approving nod as he examined Ranger's injured hoof.

"You've obviously been doing a good job keeping it clean and protected."

"Actually, Dr. Langley's been taking care of the injury," Patrick said, because he believed in giving credit where credit was due.

His grandfather's head shot up. "Are you telling me that the vet's been coming out here every day?"

"The gash was really nasty," he said in his defense. "And coronary band injuries can potentially lead to malformation and permanent hoof defects."

"You think I don't know that?" Gramps bristled. "That's why I told you to call Dr. Langley."

"I'm just trying to explain why I wanted someone with more experience and expertise overseeing Ranger's care," Patrick said.

"I'm surprised Bruce would have the time to trek out here to change a bandage." Then a speculative gleam came into the old man's eyes. "Or is it the other Dr. Langley who's been looking after your stallion?"

"It's the other Dr. Langley," he confirmed.

"Well, the girl knows her stuff," his grandfather acknowledged.

"The girl is a doctor," Patrick pointed out. "She wouldn't have graduated from veterinarian school if she didn't know her stuff."

"Graduated cum laude," Gramps informed him. "An even more impressive feat considering that she studied for her final exams with a baby at home."

"You seem to know an awful lot about Brooke Langley," he remarked.

"Of course I do. Her father and I go way back to his

early days, before that little lady was even a twinkle in his eye. Bruce is mighty proud of his girl—and the grandson who's already decided he wants to be a vet, too."

"Yeah, Brendan did mention that," Patrick said.

"You've met the boy, have you?"

"He's been out here a few times with Brooke."

"A few times?" His grandfather frowned. "I hope she keeps a close eye on him. Even if she's tending to your stock, it's not your job to babysit her kid."

"Brendan knows the rules," Patrick assured him.

"Knowing and following are two different things."

"Brendan does both. He's a good kid."

Gramps shrugged. "If you say so."

The deliberately casual response tripped an alarm in Patrick's brain. "Holy cr—" He quickly censored himself in response to his grandfather's disapproving look. "Sarah was right. You set me up."

"What are you blathering on about?"

"When Ranger was injured and you told me to call the vet, you knew it would be Brooke who came out to the ranch," Patrick accused.

"How could I possibly have known something like that?" Gramps challenged.

"I don't know," he admitted. "But I'm sure that you did."

"My only concern was for the stallion, and I'm glad to see that he's been well taken care of."

Patrick narrowed his gaze. "So you're denying that you deliberately put Brooke in my path to see if sparks would fly?"

"I've learned my lesson about interfering in the personal lives of my grandchildren," his grandfather assured him.

It was, no doubt, a reference to the separation between Patrick's cousin Brielle and Caleb Gilmore, her high school sweetheart, with whom she'd recently reunited and was expecting a child.

But it wasn't really an answer to his question.

Patrick had been looking forward to this day for three weeks, but now that it was here, he couldn't deny there was a little bit of disappointment mixed in with his relief when Brooke proclaimed Ranger's injury healed and gave permission for him to be reunited with his equine companions.

"That's great news," he said.

Except that Ranger's clean bill of health meant that Patrick would no longer get to see Brooke every day, because she'd have no reason to come out to the Silver Star.

Of course, he could ask her out on a date, but he'd tried that once already and been shot down, and he wasn't sure anything had really changed since then. Yeah, they'd shared a couple of sizzling kisses since that first encounter, but she'd firmly put on the brakes after that.

Ordinarily that would have been his cue to move on. Life was too short to waste time chasing a woman who'd clearly communicated her disinterest. Except that Brooke didn't act like she was disinterested when she was in his arms. And the memory of those kisses stirred his blood and nurtured his perhaps futile hope.

"Do you have a minute for a cup of coffee?" he asked, trying to buy some time to figure out his next move—if he was going to make one.

"I don't today," she said, sounding genuinely regretful. "I've got to get home to tackle a mountain of laundry so I can get Brendan packed and ready to go."

"Where's he going?"

"I thought he would have told you—my parents are taking him to Cedar Hills for the weekend."

"No, he didn't mention it," Patrick said. "Where's Cedar Hills and what's going on there?"

"It's a suburb of Salt Lake City where my brother and sister-in-law live with their twin daughters. It's Abbie and Zoe's tenth birthday this weekend."

"You're not going?"

She shook her head. "Someone has to be on call at the clinic. Plus, it's only a half day at school tomorrow, so they'll leave as soon as Brendan gets home and I've got appointments until four thirty."

"Are you going to be working all weekend while your parents and Brendan are away?" Patrick asked, more interested in her plans than her family's.

"Hopefully not *all* weekend," Brooke said.

For a brief moment, he thought she might be hinting that she'd have some free time so that he'd ask her out again, but her follow-up remark disabused him of that notion.

"Though I never know what kind of emergencies might arise," she pointed out.

"That must make it difficult to make plans," he commented.

"I don't make a lot of plans anyway."

Before he could decide if that was a hint, her cell phone rang.

She pulled the device out of her pocket and glanced at the screen. "Sorry, I have to take this—it's the clinic."

He stepped away to give her some privacy.

After a brief conversation, she tucked her phone away again. "And now I have another stop to make before I can get home to tackle that laundry."

He walked beside her to her truck. "Well, thanks again for everything you did for Ranger."

"Thanks for paying your bill," she said.

And then, with a smile and a wave, she was gone.

Brooke could have gone to Cedar Hills with her parents and Brendan. While it was true that someone needed to be at the clinic, there was a vet from Battle Mountain who'd covered for her father in the past—before Brooke had joined the practice—and likely would have done so again if Bruce had asked. In fact, her father had suggested just that, but Brooke wanted to prove that she was capable of caring for his patients so that he would feel comfortable taking a vacation every now and then, and maybe even retire eventually.

Sure, she was a little nervous, being the only vet on call and with her father so far away. But she also knew that she was ready for more independence and bigger challenges. And for the most part, the human clients didn't seem to mind that she was "the other Dr. Langley" so long as she was able to examine and treat their pets or other animals. And those pets, whether they had fur or feathers—or even scales—all loved her.

When she'd said goodbye to her last patient of the day, she checked her phone for a message from her parents, confirming their arrival at Kevin and Vanessa's. She sent a quick reply, adding lots of emojis for Brendan, then noticed she had another unread message— from Patrick.

Her heart skipped a beat, thinking—*hoping*—that he'd finally picked up on the hints she'd dropped about being on her own tonight.

Yeah, she still had some reservations about her ability to indulge in a good time without expectations of anything more, but she thought she was ready to give it a shot. With Patrick.

Unfortunately, his message didn't even hint at a potential good time.

I heard that a horse rolling on the ground is a sign of colic. Is this true?

She ignored the quick spurt of disappointment that he hadn't reached out in a personal capacity, because colic was a potentially serious concern—and the time stamp of the message indicated that it had been sent two hours earlier. She immediately responded.

It can be. Have you noticed any other unusual behavior?

While waiting for his reply, she expanded the cursory notes she'd made in her files earlier.

Shortly after five, Courtney poked her head in the door of Brooke's office. "Do you need me to do anything else before I go?" the vet tech asked.

"No, thanks. As soon as I finish updating this file, I'll be heading out myself."

"I can wait and walk out with you, if you're almost done," Courtney said.

"No, that's fine. It's been a long enough day already and I'm sure you've got plans tonight."

"Lowell made reservations at The Home Station," Courtney confided, naming her boyfriend.

"Special occasion?"

"Our six-month anniversary," Courtney said.

"Congratulations."

"Thanks. How about you—any special plans for the weekend?"

Brooke shook her head. "No plans at all until tomorrow morning, when I'm back here for surgeries."

"The party never stops, does it?" the vet tech teased.

"So it would seem," she agreed, returning Courtney's wave as the other woman headed out.

As Brooke finished with her notes, she found herself wondering if she'd ever been as young and carefree as her coworker. If so, she couldn't really remember because she'd had a six-month-old baby by the time she was Courtney's age. On the other hand, maybe Brendan's existence was proof that she'd not only been young and carefree, but a little bit careless, too.

After she finished her notes, she backed up the computer system and sent Patrick another quick text.

Do you want me to stop by to take a look at your horse?

She was turning into her driveway before he replied.

That would be great.

Though he didn't "sound" overly concerned, it was sometimes difficult to convey tone in a text message. But since she was already home, Brooke decided to freshen up a little before heading out to the Silver Star.

She brushed some mascara onto her lashes and slicked some gloss on her lips—then wiped the gloss off because it seemed too obvious. On second thought, maybe obvious wasn't a bad thing when trying to squeeze through a narrow window of opportunity, she decided. Because the two nights that her son would be out of town were a narrow opportunity for her to focus on being a woman rather than a mom, and one that she might not have again for a very long time. She opened the tube of gloss again, anticipation causing flutters in her tummy.

Because although she was twenty-nine years old, a certified veterinarian and a single mother of a seven-year-old son, the prospect of a romantic interlude with the handsome rancher made her feel like a giddy teenager on prom night. Not just excited but nervous, anticipating how the night would end.

And hoping it was with more than a goodbye kiss.

Was that crazy?

Was *she* crazy?

Patrick had accused her of trying to deny the chemistry between them, and he'd been right. She'd tried to ignore the attraction, but ignoring it hadn't made it go away. So she'd decided to stop pretending and acknowledge that she was ready to take the next step.

Although it was possible she was getting ahead of herself. Because if Patrick's horse was colicky, it could be a very long night for all the wrong reasons.

And worrying about the animal had her chewing the gloss off her lips again as she drove toward the Silver Star.

He must have been watching for her arrival, because the back door opened and Patrick stepped out onto the porch as soon as she pulled up beside the barn.

"Your message didn't mention which horse you're worried about," she said. "Are they stabled for the night or—"

"About that," he interjected. "I have a confession to make."

"A confession?" she echoed.

He nodded. "I sent the text in the hope of luring you out here."

She lifted a brow. "You lied about having a colicky horse?"

"I never said I had a colicky horse," he was quick to point out in his defense. "I simply asked if a horse rolling on the ground was a symptom of colic."

He was right. And it had been a clever ruse. Not that she was willing to give him any credit for it.

"But you let me believe you had a colicky horse," she said instead. "You let me worry that one of your animals was in distress."

He had the decency to look chagrined. "I'm sorry I worried you."

"But you're not sorry you lured me here under false pretenses?" she guessed.

He slid his arms around her and drew her close. "How can I be sorry when you're here?"

"But now that I know you don't have a colicky horse, there's no reason for me to stay."

"I can think of two reasons. One—you want to," Patrick said confidently. "And two—I want you to."

Because he wasn't wrong, at least about the first part, she gave up any pretense that she wasn't exactly where she wanted to be. "As it turns out, I have a confession of my own," she said.

"What's that?"

"I have an overnight bag in my truck."

His lips curved. "Do you?"

"You're surprised," she noted.

"Only because I thought I was going to have to work a lot harder to get you into my bed."

Chapter Ten

"I'm not in your bed yet," Brooke told him.

Patrick dipped his head to brush his lips along the column of her throat, raising goose bumps on her flesh, making her shiver.

"But that's where we're headed," he noted, with a smile as smug as his words.

She could hardly deny it. The fact that she was there, not just at his ranch but in his arms, proved she was committed to taking the next step.

And when he finally kissed her, the skillful mastery of his lips obliterated any lingering traces of uncertainty.

"Okay," she acknowledged, a little breathlessly, when he eased his mouth from hers. "But before we go inside, I think we should set some ground rules."

"Why?"

She would have thought the answer was obvious, but she clarified it for him now. "Because it's important that we both understand what this is and what it isn't."

He narrowed his gaze. "Is this the relationship talk?"

"No," she was quick to reply. "I'm trying to reassure you that I'm not looking for a relationship, that I don't expect one night together to turn into anything more."

"What if, after one night together, one or both of us wants more?" he challenged.

She shook her head. "That's the point in setting the boundaries now—because if one does and the other doesn't, it might lead to awkwardness or hurt feelings. But if we both agree that this one night is the beginning and the end, we can avoid that potential messiness."

"That's really what you want?" he asked, his tone dubious.

Yes.

No.

Truthfully, she wasn't sure what she wanted, but she knew she couldn't risk falling for Patrick, and the only way to be certain that wouldn't happen was to clearly define the parameters of their relationship now.

"That's the only way I can do this," she said. "The only way to ensure that Brendan won't find out."

"We're both consenting adults," he noted.

"One of us is a consenting adult with a child," she reminded him. "And I can't risk my son getting hurt."

"I would never do anything to hurt him."

"I know," she said. "But he's a little boy looking for a dad, and if he even begins to suspect there's something between us, he'll start imagining the three of us together as a family. And when that doesn't happen, he'll be hurt, despite our best intentions."

He shrugged. "Your call."

And yet something in his tone warned her that he wasn't entirely happy, which didn't make any sense to Brooke.

Why would he be annoyed that she'd specified the terms for their involvement? Wasn't no-strings sex what most guys wanted? And wasn't he the one who'd suggested having some fun and moving on?

She really didn't know, though. Her experience with the opposite sex really was limited, and even that limited experience was several years in the past, so it was entirely possible she was misreading the situation.

Deciding to focus on his words rather than his tone, she simply said "thank you" and opened the passenger door of her truck to retrieve her duffel bag.

Patrick automatically took it from her and slid his other arm across her shoulders as he guided her toward the house.

He hung her coat while she took off her boots. She'd been inside several times before, but this time, she knew they wouldn't stop at the kitchen, and the realization had the butterflies in her tummy zooming around as if they were seven-year-old boys high on sugar.

But then he did stop in the kitchen, turning to ask, "Have you had dinner?"

She shook her head. "No, but I had a late lunch."

"So you're not hungry?"

"Not for food," she said, reaching for him.

He chuckled against her lips. "I appreciate your enthusiasm, but I think I should make you something to eat first, because once I get you into bed, I plan to keep you there for a very long time."

"Promises, promises," she teased.

"I don't make a lot of promises, but those I do make, I keep," he assured her.

"Take me to bed, Patrick. I think we've both waited long enough."

He didn't make her ask again but lifted her effortlessly into his arms and carried her to the master suite at the back of the house. When he paused in the doorway, she stole a quick glance around the room, noting the neutral-colored walls, dark wood furniture and an enormous—and unmade—bed.

"I forgot to make my bed today," he admitted, a little sheepishly.

"We're just going to tangle up the sheets anyway."

"Good point," he said and tumbled with her on top of the mattress.

They'd been dancing around and toward this moment for weeks. Now that it was finally going to happen, it couldn't happen quickly enough for Brooke. She hastily unbuttoned his shirt and pushed it over his shoulders, her hands rushing to trace the taut muscles beneath.

Or maybe she was in a hurry because she was worried that, if she slowed down, she might start to think about how long it had been since she'd been naked with a man. And then she might start to worry about all the ways her body had been stretched out by pregnancy and childbirth.

Especially in comparison to his taut and sculpted body. As she ran her hands over him—happily exploring his pecs, delts and abs—she almost couldn't believe that he'd worked behind a desk for the past several years.

"You didn't build these muscles over the past few months," she said.

"When I wasn't at Blake Mining, I was usually at Crooked Creek helping my grandfather with whatever chores needed to be done," he told her.

"So maybe there's more real cowboy in you than I gave you credit for," she mused, reaching for the buckle of his belt, eager to get some of this real cowboy in her.

"I've always enjoyed working outside," he said. "Though I like to think that I do some of my best work in the bedroom."

"I think I'm going to need a demonstration," she said.

"With pleasure," he murmured.

Then he kissed her again, long and slow and deep, and she was happy to get lost in the sensual onslaught of his mouth moving over hers.

She didn't realize he'd unfastened the buttons of her shirt until he parted the fabric, pushing it over her shoulders and down her arms, trapping her hands in the sleeves behind her back, while he kissed his way down her throat and nibbled along her collarbone. She felt the rasp of the stubble on his cheeks against the soft flesh as he nuzzled the valley between her breasts.

She couldn't think straight when he was kissing her like this. She could barely think at all. And that was before he opened the center clasp of her bra and peeled back the cups, freeing her breasts.

He caught them in his hands, murmuring his approval as his thumbs began to trace circles around the already taut nipples, causing them to draw into tighter points, making her ache and yearn. She felt a similar tightening low in her belly, an almost painful coiling of tension that ached for the pleasure of release.

Then he lowered his head and captured one of those nipples in his mouth, laving the peak with his tongue, causing hot sparks to dance over her skin and liquid heat to pool between her thighs.

She'd forgotten how arousing were the contrasts between a man's body and a woman's, but every pass of his hands reminded her now. His palms were strong and calloused, a testament to the manual labor he'd been doing over the past few months, and she shivered in response to their touch.

Having freed her own hands, she explored him, too. As her fingers glided over his taut and bronzed skin, his muscles tensed and rippled. Intrigued, she leaned closer to press her lips to his chest and felt his groan reverberate through her lips.

She was hardly innocent. She'd lost her virginity almost a decade earlier. She'd carried and birthed a child. And yet she was certain she'd never been touched the way Patrick was touching her. She knew she'd never felt the way she felt in his arms.

Nothing she'd ever known or experienced before had prepared her for the intensity of the heat that pulsed in her veins. Even scarier than that realization was the uncomfortable idea nudging at the back of her mind that she might never feel the same way with anyone else. Certainly she couldn't imagine another man making her want as she wanted him.

After he'd ensured their mutual protection, he settled between her parted thighs. It had been a long time, and she wasn't prepared for his size, wincing a little as he pushed deeper inside.

He captured her mouth with his, kissing her deeply and thoroughly, until her body finally relaxed, accepting and welcoming him. Only then did he begin to move. As pleasure continued to build inside her, she lifted her hips, her heels digging into the mattress. She met him thrust for thrust, tension coiling tight in her belly. Tighter and tighter, until she finally exploded like a firework—a kaleidoscope burst of bright lights and colors—a billion tiny little shards that slowly faded as she drifted back to earth again. Patrick cried out as he found his own release, his body shuddering and then collapsing on top of her.

It was several minutes before her breathing returned to some semblance of normal.

"That was…" She trailed off, not quite sure how to finish.

"Indescribable?" he suggested.

She nodded.

"Although *wow* might also work," he decided, as he summoned the energy to roll off her.

She didn't have a chance to register and regret the loss of his weight pinning her to the mattress before he gathered her close.

"Was it *wow* for you, too?" she asked and immediately cringed at the neediness of her tone.

"Quite possibly beyond *wow*," he said.

She relaxed then, pleased by his response and grateful that she'd packed the overnight bag.

Then her stomach growled.

Audibly.

Patrick chuckled. "Now you're hungry."

"So it would seem," she agreed.

He rolled out of bed and reached for his discarded jeans. "Let's go see what I've got in the fridge."

"Apparently I need to move grocery shopping to the top of my to-do list," he commented, as he whisked eggs in a bowl.

"I don't think I even have the ingredients for an omelet in my fridge," she confided, as she stood beside him, wearing his soft flannel shirt, dicing the pepper and onion.

"That's sad," he said.

"Fortunately, if I'm really desperate, I can walk across the driveway to raid my parents' pantry."

"Is that fortunate?" he wondered.

"When you're trying to feed a growing seven-year-old boy, it's very fortunate."

Patrick poured the egg mixture into the heated pan, then chopped up some leftover ham. When the eggs were set to his satisfaction, he added the onions, peppers and ham, grated some cheese on top, expertly folded the egg in half with a spatula, then slid the omelet out of the frying pan and onto a plate.

"That can't all be for me," she protested when he set the plate in front of her.

"You're the one who didn't have dinner," he reminded her.

"But you just completed a pretty intense workout."

He smiled. "That wasn't work. That was pure pleasure."

She felt her cheeks heat and dropped her gaze to her plate, all too aware that blushing like a schoolgirl was the price of being a redhead. Picking up the fork, she cut off a piece of omelet and popped it into her mouth.

"How is it?" Patrick asked.

"Really good," she said, digging her fork into the fluffy omelet again. "So where did you learn to cook?"

"That's a rather personal question from a woman who made it clear she had no desire to complicate sex with intimacy," he remarked.

"You're annoyed that I wanted to establish some ground rules," she realized.

"I may not have a lot of experience with relationships, but I've always thought it was poor form to plan for the end at the beginning."

"I don't have a lot of experience with relationships, either," she reminded him. "And it may be that, in trying to manage my own expectations, I was a little tactless."

"Apology accepted," he said.

She smiled gratefully. "Good to know you don't hold a grudge."

"I don't want to waste the limited time we have together arguing when we could do much more interesting things."

The promise in his eyes made her insides quiver, but she refused to let him distract her from her original question. "So are you going to tell me who taught you to cook?" she asked, lifting another forkful of egg to her mouth.

"My mother."

"Really?"

"You're surprised she can cook?"

She shrugged. "I would have guessed that your family had a cook in their big house on Miners' Pass."

"My parents do have a cook, but he's only there Monday through Friday—unless they're hosting a weekend event. Otherwise, it's my mom who reigns over the kitchen on Saturdays and Sundays. She says that cooking relaxes her, and I'd agree it's the only thing that does," he confided. "She always seemed more patient in the kitchen, which is probably why I liked hanging out with her there."

"What else did she teach you how to make?"

"In addition to a simple meat loaf—"

"Simple and delicious," she interjected, reminding him that she'd already enjoyed that culinary offering.

"—I do a decent job with an omelet," he continued. "But my grilled cheese is to die for."

"To die for, huh?"

"My sister's words, not mine," he said.

"So why did I get a melt-in-your-mouth omelet instead of a to-die-for grilled cheese?" she wondered.

"They're exclusively offered on the second night," he teased. "So if you wanted to stay again tomorrow…"

"You sure know how to tempt a girl, don't you?"

she said, and she wasn't only referring to the potential sandwich. It was the man more than anything else that tempted her to throw her own rules and guidelines out the window and beg for not just a second night but as many more after that as he'd give her.

"I do my best," he said and leaned over to brush his lips over hers, tempting her even more.

"Mmm." She closed her eyes, savoring the taste of his kiss. "Now I'm craving more of your kisses."

"As it happens, I have an endless supply of those."

"Good to know," she said and drew his mouth down to hers again.

He slid his hands beneath her bottom and lifted her out of the chair. She wrapped her legs around his hips, anchoring herself to him as he made his way back to the bedroom, kissing her the whole way.

Patrick was accustomed to sleeping alone.

Though he enjoyed the pleasurable pursuits that came with sharing his bed, he generally preferred solitude for sleeping. Apparently Brooke was accustomed to sleeping alone, too, because she was sprawled in the middle of the mattress, having somehow managed to push him to the edge.

He considered waking her and nudging her on her way. He knew she wouldn't protest. Considering she was the one who'd set limitations on their relationship, she might even be relieved. But he didn't wake her, because he didn't want her to leave. He wasn't nearly ready to let her go. And that realization was more than a little disconcerting.

Or maybe he was overreacting. Maybe it wasn't surprising that, after three weeks of intense buildup, he needed more than two rounds of exceptional sex to get her out of his system.

She truly was an amazing woman—slim but toned, her muscles firm beneath silky smooth skin. An enticing contrast of softness and strength. Having watched her work with Ranger over the past few weeks, he knew she was as capable as any man, but there was no doubt that she was all woman.

He let his hand skim over her now, from calf to knee, thigh to hip, waist to breast. And, yeah, he got a little distracted there, but how could his attention not be captivated by the way her nipple immediately pebbled against his palm? How could he not be aroused to know that, even in her sleep, she responded to his touch?

He shifted closer and kissed the side of her throat; she exhaled on a sigh and rolled over so that she was facing him. Her eyes, heavy with the remnants of slumber, lifted to his.

"Did I wake you?" he asked.

Her lips curved. "I'm not sure if I'm awake or having an incredibly erotic dream."

"Let's find out," he said and lowered his head to her breast, capturing the taut nipple in his mouth.

She gasped as his tongue swirled around the rigid peak, and again when he suckled the tender flesh. He loved the sensual sounds she made, her throaty murmurs and soft sighs letting him know what she liked. She was so passionate…so incredibly responsive.

He nuzzled the hollow between her breasts, making her squirm, then kissed his way down her torso. He stroked the insides of her thighs, urging them to part, and felt her muscles quiver as she complied with his silent request.

He settled there, his broad shoulders pushing her legs farther apart, opening her to his eager gaze, his avid mouth. He touched her with his tongue, a slow, leisurely stroke. Her breath caught in her throat, then exhaled on a shuddery sigh.

He tasted her again, teasing her with his lips and his tongue until she whimpered, then licking and sucking until he heard her breath catch the way it did when she was oh so close to her release. He held her at the brink for just a moment, glorying in the power he had over her.

But of course that power was only an illusion, because he was equally in her thrall—rock hard and aching for her. He wanted nothing more than to rise up and drive himself into her, driving them both to the finish.

No, there was one thing he wanted more.

He wanted to make her come completely undone, and he wanted to watch it happen.

So he did…and it was the most beautiful thing he'd ever seen.

And when her body finally stopped shuddering with the aftershocks of her climax, he took her to the brink again. Only then did he sheathe himself with a condom and join their bodies together.

Their rhythm was easy and comfortable, as if they'd been lovers for weeks, maybe months, rather than mere hours. There was something about being with Brooke that didn't just feel familiar; it felt…right. And when she lost herself in another climax, he found his own release deep inside her.

The next time Patrick awakened, it was because Brooke was trying to disengage herself from the arm wrapped around her.

He responded by tightening his hold and pulling her closer.

She turned her head to look at him, an apologetic smile curving her lips. "I have to go."

"Why did you bother bringing an overnight bag if you didn't plan on staying overnight?"

"I did stay overnight. It's now morning."

"Not even the cows get up this early," he grumbled.

"How would you know?" she teased. "You're never up with the cows."

"Can't you stay just a little while longer?"

"I've got surgeries this morning, starting at nine o'clock," she said, sounding sincerely regretful.

He glanced at the clock. "I can work fast."

He was true to his word.

And his overnight guest left the Silver Star with a very satisfied smile on her face.

Chapter Eleven

"Someone's in a good mood today," Larissa remarked, when Brooke walked into the clinic a short while later.

"It's a bright, sunny morning," she said, grateful that she had the weather as a ready excuse. Because even if it had been gray and gloomy, she wouldn't have been able to stop smiling, and she didn't know how she would have explained her euphoria then.

She could hardly admit that she was feeling happy and relaxed because Patrick Stafford had given her multiple orgasms multiple times over the span of the ten hours she'd spent with him. Or that she'd been sincerely reluctant to leave his bed.

She wished she could have stayed.

Or that she could go back.

But she was the one who'd made the rules. She was

the one who'd insisted that one night would be enough. It didn't matter that she'd been wrong—she couldn't backtrack now.

And with Ranger's injury healed, she didn't even have the stallion as an excuse to stop by. And if Patrick sent her a vague text message about a potential problem at the ranch, she was going to ask for some specifics before she raced over there again.

Probably.

"How was your dinner at The Home Station last night?" she asked, when she found Courtney prepping the room for their first surgery.

"Amazing," the vet tech immediately replied. "And *so* romantic. The food was unbelievably good, with a different wine pairing for each course. Plus, there was candlelight and soft music."

"It sounds amazing," Brooke agreed. And though there was a part of her that hoped to dine in the fancy restaurant one day, she'd been satisfied with the omelet she'd had for dinner—and more than satisfied with everything before and after.

Thankfully, she managed to put those memories and the man out of her mind to focus on treating her animal patients. She also exchanged pleasantries with and offered reassurances to their human companions.

She had five surgeries scheduled, including two spays, a neuter, repair of a strangulated umbilical hernia in a pet lamb and the extraction of three rotted teeth from a nine-year-old Yorkshire terrier. Everything went according to plan except the second spay surgery, which she had to postpone when the pre-op exam revealed that the owners of the fifteen-month-old French bulldog had waited too long to book the procedure. Little Lulu was already pregnant.

Patrick didn't mind getting an earlier than usual start to his day. Then again, who would complain about waking up with a warm and willing woman in his arms?

In fact, he was in such a good mood, he caught himself whistling as he mucked out stalls and fed the animals. After that, he spent some time playing with the dog and even used the brush Brooke had left for grooming. Princess didn't just accept the attention but seemed to revel in it, and he found himself wondering again how anyone could have let her go.

He returned to the house to answer emails, do some banking and check the updated version of the Silver Star Vacation Ranch website—which Devin had promised would be ready to go live as soon as Patrick gave him the word. He was eager to open for business and for Melissa to arrive so they could test-drive the menu he'd drafted. Of course, Brendan had given him some input on that, too, suggesting kid-friendly additions such as French toast sticks, PB&J, mini corn dogs and a sundae bar.

Thinking of food made him realize that he hadn't eaten since lunch, and even then he'd only opened a tin of chili because he'd been too busy to make anything else. Aware of the limited contents of his refrigerator, he decided to go into town to grab a bite. Maybe he'd even reach out to a couple of friends to get together to share a couple of pizzas and a pitcher of beer.

Or maybe he'd pick up a pizza and take it over to Brooke's house.

The latter was definitely the more appealing option, except that it would be a violation of her rules.

He should be satisfied that he'd had her in his bed and move on. Except that he wasn't ready to move on, and he didn't believe she was, either. His reputation aside, he wasn't really a love-'em-and-leave-'em kind of guy. Maybe he hadn't had many long-term relationships, but he wasn't in the habit of moving directly from one woman to the next, either. Well, not since college, anyway. After his breakup with Kari, he'd perhaps been a little indiscriminate in his effort to forget her betrayal.

But that was a lot of years ago. He'd not only got over Kari, he'd moved on—again and again.

Or maybe he hadn't been as over his cheating ex as he'd wanted to believe, because although he'd dated some really great women since then, he'd never let himself get too attached to anyone. He'd never even been tempted. Until now.

Until Brooke.

It wasn't until Brooke got home and looked in the refrigerator for something to eat that she realized she'd forgotten to stop at The Trading Post. The mostly bare shelves would definitely need to be stocked before her son came home the following day, but she didn't feel up to the task of grocery shopping tonight.

Her stomach growled in protest, as if aware that she didn't have the usual option of going next door to see what her mom was cooking because her parents were out of town with Brendan. She'd been happy enough to send her son off with his grandparents because she knew he'd have a great time in Cedar Hills with his cousins. She hadn't considered how empty the apartment would seem or how lonely she'd be without him.

Of course, she hadn't really missed him the night before, because Patrick had kept her completely and thoroughly distracted. So much so that her body ached all over, and she shivered as she remembered the way he'd touched and kissed her, eliciting shockingly intense responses from her body.

But that was last night.

Tonight, she was on her own. And instead of focusing on how quiet the apartment was without her little boy, she decided to take advantage of the solitude to do the things she didn't usually do when she had a curious seven-year-old underfoot.

She started by indulging in a long bath with mountains of frothy bubbles and scented candles. She even poured herself a glass of her favorite pinot noir—or half a glass, as that was all that was left in the bottle—and savored each sip.

But then the half glass of wine started to give her bad ideas—such as texting Patrick to inquire about his not-at-all colicky horse. Thankfully, she was sober enough to realize that kind of overture might seem like a booty call.

Which, of course, it would be.

Because apparently one passion-filled night after eight years of celibacy wasn't enough for her.

Well, it was going to have to be, she admonished herself as she released the tub stopper. Because she'd made the rules and now she had to play by them.

She reached for a towel and rubbed it briskly over her body, ignoring the way her nipples tingled in response to the brush of the soft cotton, teasing her with memories of a different touch.

As she tugged on a pair of leggings and a shirt, her stomach growled again, reminding her that a half glass of wine was no substitute for dinner. She should probably go out to pick up something from Diggers' or a slice of Jo's pizza, but both options would require her to put on real clothes and leave her warm apartment, neither of which appealed to her. Which meant that she was going to have to be satisfied with frozen pizza tonight.

Brooke had just set the oven to preheat when there was a knock at the door. She didn't often get company, and nine times out of ten, when someone did knock on her door, it was either her mom or her dad. The tenth time it was usually the boy across the street, wanting to know if Brendan could come out and play.

Since she knew it couldn't be either of her parents and it was too late for Russell to be out, she peeked through the peephole before opening the door. Her heart jolted inside her chest when she identified her unexpected visitor as the cowboy of her fantasies.

She lifted a hand to push her hair—still damp from her bath—away from her face and considered pretending that she wasn't home. She definitely wasn't prepared for company. She had no makeup on and hadn't even bothered with a bra because she was alone.

Patrick knocked again, a little louder, making her realize the futility of pretending she wasn't there when her vehicle was in plain sight in the driveway. And truthfully, she really wanted to invite him in.

She unlocked the door and pulled it open.

His gaze skimmed over her, from the thick wool socks on her feet to the damp mass of hair spilling over her shoulders. "You look like you're settled in for the night," he remarked, the corners of his mouth curling with the hint of a smile.

"I wasn't expecting company," she said, hating that he'd caught her so unprepared when he looked so darn good.

"It was an observation, not a criticism," he assured her.

"What are you doing here?" she asked, her gaze shifting from the handsome man to the grocery bag he carried.

"I came into town to grab a bite and it occurred to me that, after a day of surgeries, you might not feel up to cooking."

"I didn't, which is why I was just going to throw a frozen pizza in the oven," she said.

"Or I could make you my to-die-for grilled cheese instead," he suggested.

"I thought that was a second-date meal."

"So we'll consider this our second date," he said.

She opened the door wider to allow him entry, because any kind of grilled cheese shared with the handsome cowboy was better than eating alone—especially if she could have him for dessert.

Except that they'd agreed to one night together and that night was over, she reminded herself.

So why was he here now—offering to cook for her again and calling it a second date? she challenged herself.

Oblivious to her inner struggle, Patrick held up the six-pack in his other hand. "I brought beer, too."

"Good call," she said. "Because the only beverages I could offer are tap water, milk approaching its best-before date or juice boxes."

"What kind of juice boxes?" he asked, making her smile.

"Apple, grape or fruit punch."

"I think I'll start with a beer," he decided, following her into the small kitchen and setting the grocery bag and beverages on the island.

"Do you want a glass?" she asked.

"Bottle's fine for me," he said, twisting the top off one and offering it to her.

She shook her head. "Thanks, but I already had half a glass of wine and I'm on call this weekend."

He put the bottle down and began to unpack the groceries: a loaf of twelve-grain bread, a stick of butter, three different kinds of cheese, a small bottle of honey and a plastic bag with green leaves in it.

She lifted a brow.

"I brought that from home," he said. "Because The Trading Post doesn't usually have fresh basil."

"What's the basil for?" she asked. "And the honey?"

"Why don't you sit down and relax while I make dinner?" he suggested.

"Because now my curiosity is piqued as much as my appetite," she said.

He put his hands on her shoulders and steered her toward the living room. "Go."

"You're bossy," she told him.

"And you're nosy."

Instead of arguing, she retreated to the living room to relax, as he'd suggested.

She could hear drawers and doors opening and closing as he rummaged around for the equipment he needed, but he didn't ask for help, so she didn't offer it. It was a strange experience to have someone else preparing food in her kitchen, but not an unpleasant one. And as the scent of grilled bread made its way to the living room, her stomach growled in anticipation.

A short while later, he carried a tray into the living room with sandwiches and drinks. "Is it okay to eat in here?"

"Sure," she said. "It's a little roomier and definitely more comfortable than the kitchen."

"I like your place," he said, as he set a glass of water and a plate in front of her.

"It's small," she acknowledged. "But it works for me and Brendan."

"It's cozy and warm," he countered. "And—" his gaze narrowed on the antique sideboard her mother had refinished and Brooke was using as a TV stand "—is that a Chippendale?"

She nodded. "One of my mother's flea-market finds. It was painted mint green when she brought it home."

"She's got a good eye," he remarked.

"So do you," Brooke noted. "Not a lot of guys recognize specific furniture styles."

"My parents have a lot of Chippendale furniture at their place," he said.

And not a single piece that had come from a flea market, Brooke surmised, as she lifted half of the grilled cheese to her mouth and took a bite.

"Ohmygod." She closed her eyes as she chewed, savoring the contrasting flavors and textures, with just a hint of sweetness. "This is *sooo* good."

"That's what you said last night," he said.

Her eyes popped open then, and he winked boldly, making her blush.

"I did not," she protested, though she wasn't entirely sure she hadn't.

"Maybe not in those words," he said. "But I read between the lines of your moans and whimpers."

"Then I guess it's a good thing you don't have to worry about listening to a repeat performance," she responded in a prim tone.

He grinned, unrepentant. "What if I said that I love the noises you make when I touch you? That they're an incredible turn-on? And that I've been walking around in a semi-aroused state all day thinking about your body shuddering beneath mine?"

"I'd think that maybe this grilled cheese was just a prelude to a booty call," she said. "Was it?"

"That's entirely up to you," he said. "But since you made it clear that you weren't going to come back out to the Silver Star tonight, I thought I'd come here."

"You have to know it isn't location that's the problem."

"After last night, I'm having a little trouble believing that there *is* a problem."

"I'm not the kind of woman who has affairs, Patrick."

"Yeah, you mentioned that once or twice before," he said.

"And you're not the kind of man who does relationships," she said.

"Not according to the rumor mill in town," he agreed.

"And as a single mom of an impressionable seven-year-old son, I don't want to add any grist to that mill."

"I know how to be discreet, if that's your concern," he assured her.

"Patrick, you can be with any woman you want."

"And I want you," he said.

She sighed, both flattered and frustrated by his obstinacy. "Do you really? Or do you just want to be the one who walks away when a relationship is over?"

"Trust me," he said. "This isn't about ego. It's about attraction. I'm here now because I still want you so much I can't seem to think about anything else."

"Trust doesn't come easily to me," she admitted.

"He really did a number on you, didn't he?"

Brooke knew he was referring again to the man who'd got her pregnant. And though she really didn't want to discuss her romantic history—limited though it was—she realized that telling him at least a little bit about her past might be the easiest way to make him understand why she was so wary.

"He wasn't the only one," she said. "Every time I've let myself rely on a man, I've been let down. And not just in romantic relationships, either."

"Tell me," he said. "I'll take names, track them down and beat them up."

She smiled at that. "Well, first there was Hayden Reed, who, in fourth grade, offered to trade his yogurt tube for my string cheese and then ate both snacks."

"We're going back that far, are we?" he remarked, sounding amused.

"You asked," she reminded him. "Next came Christian Harvick, my lab partner in biology, who didn't bother to do his part of our joint assignment, forcing me to do it so we both didn't get a zero. Then Mr. Olerud, the high school volleyball coach."

"I remember Mr. Olerud," he said.

"He cut me from the team in my junior year in favor of a transfer student, not because Analise was a better player than me but because her father offered to buy new uniforms for the team."

"That sucks," he agreed.

But she wasn't done yet.

"Dr. Etherington was one of my professors at college," she continued. "He docked me five marks for throwing up during a dissection when I was ten weeks pregnant, because if I couldn't stomach the job, I shouldn't be there.

"And then there's my brother Nathan—a plastic surgeon in LA—who changed his mind about coming to Brendan's baptism at the eleventh hour because an A-list celebrity wanted a consult. On a Sunday afternoon."

"I'm sorry," he said sincerely.

"Kevin and Vanessa—my other brother and sister-in-law—were there, though. Proudly standing up as godparents for their nephew, along with my best friend, Lori. And my parents, of course." She set her empty plate on the table. "My dad's the one man who's always been there for me."

"I can see why you have some trust issues," he acknowledged. "But you can count on me, Brooke. Because I won't ever make you any promises I don't intend to keep."

And maybe, for right now, that was enough, Brooke thought, as he dipped his head to touch his mouth to hers.

Because right now, she wanted him as much as he wanted her. More. She parted her lips for the searching thrust of his tongue, her fingers digging into his strong, broad shoulders, holding on to him for balance as the world tilted and spun. And that was before his hands slid under her top, and he groaned against her lips when he found her breasts unfettered. He cupped them in his palms, his thumbs teasing her nipples so that she whimpered.

"If you want me to go, tell me now," he urged.

"I don't want you to go," she admitted. "But you can't leave your truck in my driveway all night."

"I'd ask if you have nosy neighbors, but this is Haven and you have neighbors, so enough said."

She nodded, grateful for his understanding.

"What time do I have to leave to minimize the gossip?" he asked.

"You don't have to leave. You just have to park in the garage."

"I'll be right back," he promised.

* * *

After they made love, Brooke drifted off in his arms. And while Patrick was happy to hold her, his stomach was thinking it wanted another sandwich. Carefully untangling their limbs, he slipped out of her bed, pulling the covers up over her so she wouldn't get cold in his absence.

He was sliding the grilled cheese out of the frying pan and onto a plate when she appeared in the kitchen. Her eyes were sleepy, her hair disheveled, and while he hadn't really expected that she would wander through her apartment naked, he was disappointed to see that she'd pulled an oversize T-shirt on to cover up her sexy body.

"I was hungry," he said, as he sliced the sandwich in half.

"And I was thirsty," she told him.

"Do you want half of this?" he offered.

"No, thanks," she said, reaching into the cupboard for a glass.

As she stretched, the hem of that T-shirt rode enticingly high on her thighs, and he felt his body stir. Was it normal, he wondered, to want a woman the way he wanted her? Or had she somehow entranced him?

He scowled at the thought as he bit into his sandwich.

"Although I meant to tell you that I agree with your sister," she said, as she filled her glass from the pitcher in the fridge. "You do make a to-die-for grilled cheese.

"In fact, I was thinking that if you're not successful in finding a cook for the Silver Star, you could handle the kitchen duties yourself. Omelets for breakfast, grilled cheese for lunch and meat loaf for dinner."

"Lucky for my guests, I did find a cook."

"You did?"

He chewed another bite of sandwich. "And not just any cook, but a graduate of the International Culinary Center in New York currently working at a fancy restaurant in Seattle."

"How'd you snag someone with those credentials?" she wondered.

"Melissa's my cousin."

"Ah." Brooke nodded. "So when's she coming to Haven?"

"She gave her two weeks' notice last week, so I'd guess she'll be here sometime the week after next."

"You *guess*? Most people in business like to firm up those kinds of details."

"I'm not worried," he said. "There's still lots of time before Memorial Day weekend."

"So you've picked the date for your grand opening?"

He nodded.

"That's fabulous news," she said.

"In other news—" he set his empty plate aside and reached for her, drawing her into his arms "—my hunger for food has been satisfied, but not my desire for you."

"Maybe it's a proximity thing," she said.

"You're suggesting that I only want you because you're here and looking sexy as hell in an old T-shirt?"

She glanced down at the T-shirt. "Or maybe you're

under the influence of alcohol," she allowed. "How many beers did you have?"

"Just one."

"You're a cheap date."

"And easy," he promised.

She smiled at that. "You're going to let me have my way with you?"

"You can have me any way you want, anytime," he promised.

Her speculative gleam shifted to something else when a ringing sound emanated from the iPad on the counter.

"It's a FaceTime call," Brooke told him. "Probably Lori calling me back."

She'd reached out to her friend earlier, wanting to tell her about the events of the previous night and seek her advice on what to do next. Since then, Patrick had answered that question for her. Of course, Lori couldn't know that, and Brooke's message had asked her to call whenever she got in, because Brooke had anticipated being home alone all night.

"Don't you want to talk to her?" he asked, when Brooke made no move to answer.

"I do, but…"

"I promise to stay hidden from the camera," he said, anticipating her concern.

So she reached for her iPad and connected the call.

After a brief exchange of pleasantries, she listened for several minutes as her friend told her about the fabulous day she'd spent with Matt, who'd just popped out to pick up pizza for a late snack. Then Lori stopped talking midsentence and narrowed her gaze on the screen. "Oh. My. God," she said. "You've had sex."

"What?" Brooke tried to feign ignorance, as if she had no idea why her friend had jumped to such a conclusion, but she suspected that her burning cheeks had already confirmed Lori's suspicion.

"Don't you dare try to deny it. I've seen that sleepy, satisfied look in your eyes in my own mirror to know what puts it there," Lori said. "Not to mention the redness on your throat that suggests up close and personal attention from a man's bristly jaw."

"Okay, yes," she finally admitted, aware that Patrick was within earshot but not daring to look at him. "I had sex."

"Really good sex?" her friend asked hopefully.

Brooke felt her cheeks burn hotter.

"Tell me," Lori urged. "And don't spare any of the juicy details."

"I can't. Not now," she said.

"Why not?" And then her friend's eyes grew even wider. "Oh. My. God," she said again. "He's still there, isn't he? Whoever *he* is."

Brooke closed her eyes on a sigh. "Yes, he's still here."

"Who is it? Anyone I know? Can you turn the camera so I can see him?"

"Not telling, maybe and no," she said, answering each of the questions in turn.

"Okay, don't tell me," Lori said. "But don't be surprised when I come for a visit to meet your new boy toy."

"He's not— It's not—" She huffed out a breath.

Her friend grinned, obviously amused by Brooke's flustration.

"Pizza's here!" Matt called from off-camera.

Lori twisted her head to respond to the summons. "I'm coming." Then she returned her attention to the screen and, with a wink, said to Brooke, "And hopefully you'll be saying the same thing in short order."

Thankfully she cut the connection before her friend heard Patrick choke on a laugh.

Chapter Twelve

"Sneaking out of bed when a man's still sleeping could give him a complex, you know," Patrick said, squinting against the bright light that speared through the gap between Brooke's bedroom curtains.

"Obviously you're not sleeping, or we wouldn't be having this conversation," Brooke responded, as she found her discarded T-shirt on the floor and tugged it over her head.

"I'd like to be sleeping," he said.

She yanked the curtains together to shut out the blinding light.

"With you," he clarified.

She shook her head regretfully. "Brendan's going to be home in a few hours and I have a million errands to run before then, including grocery shopping so I have some food in the house to feed my child."

He sighed. "I've got things to do, too, but nothing that would be nearly as much fun as staying in bed with you."

"I'm sorry," she said and touched her lips to his. "And thank you."

"You're welcome. But why are you thanking me?"

"Because this weekend was the first time I've been away from Brendan for so long, and I thought I'd hate every minute of it. But, thanks to you, I didn't."

"Your flattery is overwhelming," he said dryly.

"I didn't think you needed me to further pump up your already inflated ego."

"I should have stopped with the 'you're welcome,'" he decided.

She brushed her lips against his again. "Thank you, too, for the orgasms."

He grinned. "Anytime."

But she shook her head again.

"That's right—you're done with me now," he said, only half joking.

"I have a child," she reminded him.

"I have no desire or intention to compete with your son for your attention," he assured her. "But in addition to being a veterinarian and a mom, you are an amazing and sensual woman, Brooke. And while I understand that Brendan comes first, that doesn't mean you can't make time for other things or other people who matter. Including yourself."

"Between my job and my son, I don't have a lot of time for anything—or anyone—else," she confided.

"I'm not asking for more than you're willing to give," he said. "Just that you think about me, and when you have some time, you consider spending it with me."

"That sounds rather vague." And, she had to admit, infinitely reasonable.

"Would you prefer that I made irrational demands so that you'd feel better about refusing them?"

"Of course not," she denied. "But what if a couple of weeks go by and I haven't managed to find any time for you?"

"I do have my own life and responsibilities," he reminded her, pushing back the covers and rising out of the bed, completely unconcerned about his nakedness.

"I know that," she said, trying not to stare—and failing happily. "I also know you're accustomed to a...busy social calendar." She flushed a little.

"Not only have you been listening to gossip, it's outdated." He gathered up his clothes and began to dress. "Maybe I've dated a lot of women in the past, but since I bought the Silver Star, I've spent most of my nights there. Alone."

"You had a lot of work to do, updating and renovating the property," she pointed out. "But that's all done now, so you'll have more free time on your hands."

"And how else would I fill that time except by seducing all the single women in town?" he asked dryly.

Now her cheeks flamed. "You're deliberately misunderstanding me."

"I don't think I'm misunderstanding anything, and

I don't know whether to be pissed that you have such a low opinion of me or that you don't think more of your-self to trust I'd want to be with you."

Either way, he sounded pretty pissed.

And maybe he had a right to be.

Maybe she had judged him unfairly.

But this fling or affair or whatever he wanted to call it was outside her realm of experience. She didn't know what to say or do the "morning after" because she didn't *do* mornings after.

"So what do you want me to say? Is this where I'm supposed to apologize?" she asked him now.

"No," he said. "I want you to figure out what you want. When you do, you can let me know."

Brendan was happy to be home and eager to share all the details of his exciting weekend. He'd obviously enjoyed the trip and entertained everyone with his chat-ter throughout the meal Brooke had prepared for their return.

"So how was your weekend?" Sandra asked, when Brendan had finally tired himself out from talking and gone into the living room to watch TV with Grandpa.

"It was good."

"I hope you didn't spend every minute at the clinic."

She shook her head. "Only Saturday. The rest of the weekend was fairly quiet."

"So what did you do with your time otherwise?"

She could have replied in any number of ways that would have answered her mother's question without telling her the whole truth, but she really needed some womanly advice right now. "I spent some of it at the Silver Star. With Patrick."

"Oh." Her mom considered this revelation for a moment, then nodded. "Well, then. Good for you."

Brooke didn't know what kind of response she'd expected from her mother, but she was a little surprised by her easy acceptance. "You don't think I'm making a mistake?"

"Why? Because you're finally taking steps toward having a life of your own aside from your career and your child?"

"Brendan will always be my number one priority," she was quick to assure her mom.

"And that's okay," Sandra said. "But he shouldn't be the focus of your whole life. That's not healthy for you and not fair to him."

Brooke frowned at the subtle admonishment. "I feel as if I owe him at least that much."

"Why?" her mom asked, then immediately guessed the answer to her own question. "Because he has only one parent?"

She nodded. "I know he lucked out in the grandparent department, but I'm not sure that makes up for the absence of a father in a little boy's life."

"It's not your fault that you fell in love with a man who didn't want the responsibility of being a father," Sandra said gently.

"Maybe not the first time," Brooke agreed, having long ago come to terms with the fact that she'd been too young and naive to know any better when she'd fallen for Xander Davis. "But what if I'm doing the same thing again?"

"Are you telling me that you're in love with Patrick Stafford?" Sandra asked cautiously.

"No," she immediately denied. "But…I do have feelings for him. And the more time I spend with him, the stronger those feelings seem to get, making me worry that I could fall in love with him."

"Falling in love should be cause for celebration, not concern," her mom pointed out.

Maybe. In a perfect world.

But in Brooke's imperfect world, opening up her heart had only led to heartache, and it wasn't an experience she was eager to repeat. Especially if it meant risking her son, too.

Thankfully, with Brendan home, life returned to normal for Brooke. She easily fell back into her usual routines, almost as if the two glorious nights she'd spent with Patrick had never happened.

Monday was her usual full day at the clinic. Tuesday she was occupied with fieldwork in the morning and had surgeries in the afternoon, but she finished early enough that she was actually home by the time Brendan got off the bus from school.

On Wednesday, Brooke spent the better part of the day beside her dad at Ambling Acres, each of them up to their respective elbows in bovine butts, determining which cows were pregnant and which were in heat and ready to be bred. It was hardly a glamorous job, but she always enjoyed being in the field with her father.

Though she'd studied hard and graduated near the top of her class, she knew there were a lot of things that could only be learned from experience, and Bruce Langley had close to forty years' experience.

On Thursday, she visited a local sheep farm to administer routine vaccinations, after which she was invited to share lunch with the farmer and his wife. She considered the personal connection between vet and landowner to be one of the perks of a rural practice and was happy to accept. On her way back to the clinic, she impulsively turned into the drive of the Silver Star, only to discover that Patrick's truck wasn't there. He'd told her to let him know when she'd figured out what she wanted, but she found herself wondering now if he might have already given up on hearing from her.

Friday morning after breakfast, she took Brendan over to her parents' house to wish them a happy anniversary and give them a gift certificate to The Home Station, where she'd made a six o'clock reservation for them to celebrate the occasion. Hugs and kisses were exchanged all around. Then Brooke hustled her son outside again to ensure he didn't miss the school bus.

"But what are we gonna do for dinner for the 'versary?" Brendan asked, apparently having only now realized that his grandparents had plans that didn't include him.

"I thought we could go out to eat tonight, too," she told him. "But probably somewhere a little less fancy."

"Jo's?" he asked hopefully.

"We can go to Jo's," she agreed.

"Yay!" he enthused, with a celebratory fist pump.

"And after dinner, we can go see a movie, if you want."

"The-new-*Star-Wars*-is-playing," he said, rushing the words together in his excitement.

She chuckled. "I guess that's a yes to the movie?"

"I've been waiting to see it *for-ev-er*," he told her.

"The movie only came out before Christmas, so if three months is *for-ev-er*, I marvel over the fact that you survived."

He giggled at that and threw his arms around her to give her a quick hug as the yellow bus came to a stop at the end of the driveway.

She kissed the top of his head—or at least the pom-pom on his hat. "Have a good day, sunshine."

"Love you, Mom."

Though the words had become a part of their morning routine, they never failed to fill her with joy, and she was smiling as she watched him step through the folding door. He made his way down the center aisle of the bus to his usual seat, then turned to the window and offered her a happy wave.

As she drove to the clinic, she found herself reflecting on her parents' marriage. Growing up, she'd taken it for granted that when she was ready to settle down, she'd meet the perfect man, fall in love, get married and start a family. And though her life had taken a different direction, she hadn't entirely given up hope that she might one day meet a man who would love her and her son as much as her father loved her mother and their children.

Or maybe she'd already met him.

She shook her head, immediately dismissing the thought.

Patrick Stafford was definitely *not* the type of man about whom she should be imagining happily-ever-after fantasies. Sexual fantasies, sure. And in the five nights since he'd left her bed, she'd indulged in more than a few of those. But it was time to get her head and her heart out of the clouds and back into the real world.

Because despite his request that she think about him, which she'd done every night when she went to bed alone and more than a few times throughout each day, he'd given no indication that he'd been thinking about her. Not one phone call or even a text message throughout the whole week. And the silence was a little disconcerting.

Was he respecting her boundaries, abiding by her request not to turn their weekend tryst into anything more? Was he waiting for her to make the next move, as he'd encouraged her to do? Or had he already moved on?

And why did the latter possibility leave her feeling so empty inside?

It took every ounce of willpower Patrick possessed not to pick up the phone and call Brooke during the week, but he'd made it clear what he wanted and left the ball in her court. Unfortunately, she'd given no indication that she intended to return to the game, and he was admittedly a little disappointed.

"Why are you in such a grumpy mood?" Jenna asked, when she stopped by the ranch Friday afternoon.

"I'm not grumpy. I'm busy," he told her.

She didn't take the hint.

"Is this about the sexy vet?" she asked instead.

He scowled. "What are you talking about?"

"Sarah told me that you've got the hots for the new vet who was taking care of Ranger," she said. "And now that his injury is healed, there's no reason for her to stop by every day."

"The important part of that is that Ranger's injury is healed," he said.

"I know it's a little old-fashioned," she continued, as if he hadn't spoken, "but if you want to see her, you could call her and invite her to go on a date."

"Is that why you're hanging around here—because you don't have a date tonight?"

"I could have made plans if I'd wanted to," she said, just a little defensively. "And I'll bet, if you bothered to scroll through the contact list in your phone, you could, too."

"I've got things to do around here tonight," he said.

"What kinds of things?" she challenged.

"Are you offering to help?" he asked her.

"No," she said. "I'm calling out your obvious lie."

He scowled at that.

"Look around, Patrick. You've done an incredible job with this ranch. But you're done. Everything is ready. You just need to give Devin the word to make the website live."

"It's not really that simple," he said.

"Of course it is," she said. "But something's holding you back, and I can't figure out if it's a fear of success or failure."

"Why would I be afraid of success?"

"That's a good question," she said and waited for him to come up with an answer.

He sighed. "Maybe I am a little worried that, after spending so much time and money on this ranch, it might turn out that Mom and Dad were right," he acknowledged.

"Does that mean you're ready to throw in the towel and go back to your corner office at Blake Mining, where you can be unhappy for the rest of your life?"

"No," he said. Because she was right. He'd been not only restless but unhappy in the corporate world. But working on the ranch, he felt fulfilled and content. And, yes, happy.

"You've certainly seemed a lot happier since you moved out here—and even more so the past several weeks," she noted.

"It is a relief to know that most of the major work is done."

"Do you really think that's all it is?" she asked.

"Obviously you have a different theory."

"I do," Jenna confirmed. "And her name is Brooke."

Patrick just shook his head, unwilling to discuss his relationship with Brooke—if it could even be called a relationship—with his sister.

"I'm going into town to grab a pizza," he abruptly decided. "Do you want to come with me?"

"No, I think I'll hang out with Princess for a while."

"Okay."

"Hey," she said, as he started to turn away. "If it's okay, I think I'll crash here tonight."

"Sure," he said, because he knew she was only sharing her plans and not really asking permission. Then, because the question had been nudging at the back of his mind for a few weeks now, he asked, "Is everything okay with you and Nate?"

"We're going through a bit of a rough patch," she said.

"Do you want me to stay home tonight?"

That earned him a scowl. "Definitely not. I don't need a babysitter."

"Okay," he relented.

But as he drove into town, it occurred to him that his sister had been spending a lot of time at the ranch lately, making him suspect that the "rough patch" she'd mentioned might be more than that.

It was only a fleeting thought, though, as his mind was more preoccupied with her comment about Brooke. Because whether or not he was willing to admit it, it was true that his happiest days had been the ones he'd spent with the sexy vet—and her son.

On the way to Jo's Friday night, Brooke resolved to put all thoughts of Patrick out of her mind and focus on enjoying her son's company. That resolution lasted only until they walked into the restaurant and she saw the rancher leaning on the counter by the cash register, chatting up the very young and very pretty girl working there.

She ignored the jolt of awareness that surged through her body, leaving high-voltage tingles humming through her veins, even as she cursed herself for the instinctive response.

"Why don't we take one of those tables over there?" she suggested, attempting to steer her son away from the counter before he spotted Patrick.

But she wasn't quick enough.

"Hey, it's Mr. Patrick," Brendan said and immediately began waving. "Hi, Mr. Patrick."

The rancher glanced over and his mouth—the same mouth that had kissed her until they were both breathless and then done other and more interesting things to other parts of her—curved into an easy smile for her son. "Hey, Brendan." Then Patrick's attention shifted to Brooke, and even from across the room, she felt the heat of his gaze as his eyes skimmed over her in what could only be described as a visual caress. "Dr. Langley."

She inclined her head in acknowledgment. "Mr. Stafford," she said, inwardly wincing at the primness of her own tone.

He said something else to the girl behind the counter, then sauntered over to the table where she and Brendan were now seated. He didn't wait for an invitation but straddled an empty chair and flashed another of those bone-melting smiles. "Small world, huh?"

"Small town," she clarified. Though she managed a lighter tone this time, she was helpless to rein in her galloping pulse. Apparently her traitorous body hadn't got the memo from her brain that she was supposed to be over him.

"We're gonna have pizza for dinner," Brendan chimed in, unwilling to be left out of the conversation.

"Then you came to the right place," Patrick said, with a wink for the boy as a server approached the table.

Brooke ordered a diet cola for herself and root beer for Brendan, plus their usual pizza—a medium with cheese and pepperoni, since Brendan didn't really like any other toppings on his pie.

"I'll be right back with your drinks," the server promised. "And your pizza will be ready to go in just a few minutes, Mr. Stafford."

"Can I change it to eat-in rather than take-out?" he asked.

"Of course," she responded.

"Great. And I'll take a root beer, too." He flashed his devastating smile in the server's direction, flustering the poor girl so much that her notepad and pen slipped from her fingers.

He scooped both items off the floor and returned them to her. "You can add the soda and Dr. Langley's order to my tab."

"No," Brooke immediately protested. "Don't add…" Her words trailed off as she realized the server was already hurrying away to do his bidding—and maybe to splash some cold water on her flushed cheeks.

So Brooke directed her attention—and ire—at Patrick. "I'm not letting you buy our dinner."

"I know we're doing things a little out of order," he said. "Usually I buy a woman dinner first, but better late than never, right?"

She frowned in disapproval of his not-so-veiled reference to the nights they'd spent together. Thankfully, her son was oblivious to the implications of Patrick's remark as well as the undercurrents between the adults.

The server returned almost immediately with their drinks and three plates, and then with Patrick's pizza, which she set on an elevated stand in the middle of the table.

Brendan eyed the pie hungrily.

"Go ahead and dig in," Patrick urged.

But Brooke shook her head. "He doesn't like mushrooms."

"It's lucky, then, that they're only on the top and easy to pick off." He lifted a slice from the pan and set it on the boy's plate. "Careful, though. It's pretty hot," he cautioned, as he transferred a second slice to Brooke's plate before taking one for himself.

To her surprise, conversation didn't lag at all while they ate. The even bigger surprise was that it was Patrick and Brendan who mostly kept it going.

Despite his long-ago claim that he had no interest in kids, the rancher spent a lot of time not just talking to her son but actively engaging him on a variety of topics. Of course, he and Brendan had become pretty well acquainted after "consulting" during several visits at the Silver Star, but Brooke was still surprised by the easy flow of their conversation.

In between bites of pizza and sips of root beer, they talked about Ranger and Princess, discussed Brendan's favorite and least favorite subjects at school (phys ed and history, respectively), and somehow ended up in a DC versus Marvel debate, comparing both comic book story lines and movie adaptations. And Brooke noticed that when her son helped himself to a second slice of Patrick's pizza, he didn't even bother to peel the mushrooms off the top.

Of course, two pieces were all he wanted, and he was finished eating before the pie that she'd ordered was delivered to the table.

"Can I go play video games with Russell?" Brendan asked, having spotted his friend by one of the vintage machines at the back of the restaurant. The games were a recent addition to Jo's, introducing *Pac-Man*, *Frogger* and *Tetris* to a whole new generation of kids.

Brooke dug a couple of quarters out of her wallet and handed them to her son.

"Does he ever slow down?" Patrick asked, watching as Brendan raced across the room to the machines.

"Only when he's asleep," she said, a smile touching her lips.

"How long will the games keep him occupied?" he wondered.

"We'll see." She watched the boys slide their coins into the machines and take their positions before shifting her attention back to Patrick. "But there's no reason for you to stick around."

"I'm hoping if I do, I'll get dessert," he said.

Of course, they both knew there weren't any desserts on Jo's menu.

So why was he looking at her as if she was a slice of Twelve-Layer Chocolate Bliss that he wanted to savor?

Chapter Thirteen

Brooke lifted her glass and swallowed a mouthful of soda, hoping the icy beverage would cool that heat that rushed to fill her cheeks. "It's a Friday night," she pointed out. "Don't you have a date or something?"

"There is a woman I'm interested in," Patrick acknowledged. "But she keeps trying to brush me off."

"Maybe you should take the hint."

"I thought about it," he said. "I mean, there are plenty of other single women in this town."

"So why aren't you with one of them?" she pressed, ignoring the stab of something that felt uncomfortably like jealousy.

"Because it occurred to me that maybe I'm being pushed away by this woman not because she doesn't want me but because she's afraid to admit how much she wants me."

"You really do have an impressive...ego."

He grinned. "Yes, she did seem to be impressed by my...ego...last weekend."

She rolled her eyes at that even as her body stirred in response to the memories.

Then his smile faded and his expression turned serious. "I missed you this week."

She swallowed and mentally trampled the blossom of hope that sprang to life inside her. "Did you?"

"You have no idea how many times I picked up the phone to call you."

"And yet my phone never rang," she noted.

"You were supposed to let me know when you'd figured out what you wanted," he reminded her.

"But it's not just about what *I* want," she said. "It can't be."

"Brendan doesn't seem to mind hanging out with me."

"Brendan is a kid desperately looking for a father figure."

"You're trying to scare me off."

"Maybe I am," she conceded. "But I'm also being honest."

"I'm trying to be honest, too," he said. "And I know you said you didn't want to have an affair or a fling or anything else, but since I met you, I haven't wanted to be with anyone else. I haven't thought about anyone else. So maybe we should give the relationship option a shot."

"Oh." She didn't seem to know what else to say.

She hadn't let herself believe that he might want anything more than what they'd already shared together. Because a relationship was somehow a lot more intimate than sex, and a lot more terrifying.

He lifted a brow. "Is that all you're going to say?"

"I don't know what else to say," she admitted. "Except... maybe...do you want to go see a movie with us tonight?"

"I'd love to," he said, as Brendan headed back to the table.

"Aren't you going to ask what movie?"

"Doesn't matter."

But Brendan chimed in again. "We're gonna see the new *Star Wars* movie."

"I didn't know there was a new *Star Wars* movie," Patrick said.

"It's only 'new' in that we haven't yet seen it and it's finally showing at Mann's," Brooke clarified, naming the local second-run theater.

"Have you seen it?" Brendan asked. "Is it totally awesome?"

"I've heard that it is, but, no, I haven't seen it," Patrick admitted.

"You could see it with us," her son immediately offered. "That would be okay, wouldn't it, Mom?"

"I've already invited Mr. Patrick to come with us," she said.

"Did you say 'yes'?" Brendan asked him.

"I said 'yes,'" Patrick confirmed. "I'll even spring for the popcorn."

"You paid for the pizza," Brooke pointed out. "I'll get the popcorn."

"Why don't we compromise?" he suggested. "You can get the tickets and I'll get the snacks, because I want Milk Duds with my popcorn."

"Can we get gummy bears, too?" Brendan asked, when they were in line at the concession stand a short while later.

"How can you want candy after two slices of pizza?" Brooke wondered.

"I'm growing like a weed," he said, quoting her oft-repeated sentiment.

"Which is the only reason I agreed to the popcorn," she told him, as Patrick hid a smile.

"But I like to mix gummy bears in my popcorn."

"Gummy bears *and* Milk Duds are even better," Patrick said.

Brooke made a face. "Please tell me you don't seriously mix candy with your popcorn."

"If I told you that, it would be a lie," he confided.

"Clearly you have the taste buds of a seven-year-old."

"I do have a sweet tooth," he acknowledged, then dipped his head to whisper close to her ear, "That's why I like you."

"Can I get a blue raspberry slushy?" Brendan asked, proving once again that he was paying no attention to their conversation.

Patrick looked at Brooke, seeking her approval before acquiescing to her son's request.

She started to open her mouth to protest that Brendan had already had soda with dinner, but closed it again without saying a word. Though she didn't approve of him overloading on sugar, a night out at the movies was a special occasion and she didn't think it would hurt him too much to indulge a little. But she did caution, "If you want another drink, you better make sure you go to the bathroom before the movie starts."

"I'll go now," Brendan said and dashed off.

She didn't usually let him go off on his own when they were in a crowd, but the entrance and exit of the facilities were visible from where she was standing—and even closer to the condiment bar.

"I'll get straws and napkins," she said, leaving Patrick to wait for their snacks at the counter.

She was occupied for less than a minute, but when she turned back again, she saw that Patrick had both hands on a cardboard tray, a woman hanging off his arm and a smear of peach lipstick beside his mouth. And for one quick moment, she flashed back to college.

She'd felt so lucky to be with Xander, who was so incredibly handsome and charming and popular. And she hadn't worried about the other girls who were always flirting with him, because he'd chosen to be with her and only her. It was what he'd always told her. And what she'd believed—until she'd found him in bed with her roommate.

But Patrick wasn't Xander, and she had no reason to resent the attention he was getting from the other woman or want to yank him away from the female who was now leaning close to whisper in his ear.

To his credit, Patrick didn't look at the cleavage on display by the woman's V-neck sweater. In fact, he seemed to be looking everywhere else and exhaled visibly with relief when his gaze connected with Brooke's.

The pouting brunette, clearly unhappy with the lack of attention she was getting, tugged on his arm to draw his focus back to her again.

Patrick shook his head in response to whatever she'd said, and she finally released his arm and turned to rejoin a group of friends waiting for concessions.

As he approached, Brooke plucked another paper napkin from the dispenser and offered it to him. "You might want to wipe off the lipstick. That shade doesn't really work with your skin tone."

He set the tray down on the edge of the counter to take the napkin from her. "That was Nikki," he said, as he scrubbed his cheek. "We went out a few times, a couple of years ago."

"You don't owe me any explanations," she assured him.

"I think I'd want an explanation if I saw one of your ex-boyfriends kissing you when we were out on a date together."

"An unlikely scenario considering that the number of my ex-boyfriends can be counted on one hand," she said. "And also, this isn't a date."

"Enjoying a movie and sharing popcorn counts as a date in my books," he said.

"I can guarantee I won't be sharing that popcorn if you put gummy bears and Milk Duds in it," she said.

"It's still a date."

"With a seven-year-old chaperone?"

He shrugged. "Dating a single mom is a new experience for me, but I'd guess child-age chaperones are fairly common."

"Which is another reason you might prefer to watch the movie with Nikki."

"I already told her I wasn't interested or available because I was seeing somebody else."

"Inviting you to join me and Brendan at the movies doesn't mean we're seeing each other," she said.

"How about more than eighteen hours naked together?" he challenged. "What does that mean?"

Before she could figure out an answer to his question, Brendan was back, wiping his damp hands down the front of his jeans.

"There are dryers in the bathroom," she pointed out to her son.

"They take too long and I don't want to miss any previews," Brendan said.

"And on the plus side, at least you know he washed," Patrick said.

Since she couldn't deny the truth of that, she only said, "Let's go find some seats."

It wasn't a date.

Patrick's claims to the contrary aside, Brooke was certain of that.

And yet, when their fingers touched inside the bucket of popcorn (because, yes, she couldn't resist the salty treat, despite the candy he'd tossed inside—to her son's delight), tingles ran up her arm and memories of his strong hands moving over her flooded her brain and heated her body. And when he leaned close to whisper to her, he let his lips skim the outer shell of her ear, making her shiver. And when the theater was dark and the popcorn was gone, he linked their fingers together and held her hand.

It was both an unexpected and sweet gesture, and it made her realize how much she'd missed out on by not dating in high school and then falling for the wrong guy in college. Maybe it was her inexperience that made her susceptible to Xander's seduction, or maybe he'd been every bit as charming as she'd imagined, but she'd fallen hard and fast, and then she'd fallen into his bed.

Looking back, it was hard to pinpoint the reasons for her infatuation with Xander. During their whirlwind courtship, he'd never shown up at her door with food just because he thought she might have had a difficult day or cooked for her when she'd had to work late on an assignment. He'd never even taken her to a movie. And while those were all little things, they added up to a lot.

The fact that Xander had never done any of those things proved that she'd devoted far too much time and energy to a relationship that was a lot of nothing. But of course Xander's biggest failing was that he'd never shown any interest in his child, instead choosing to drop out of her life before their baby was even born.

She'd been holding herself back from Patrick because she'd thought he was like Xander, but she realized now that any similarities were only on the surface. Yes, both men were handsome and charming and had turned her inside out with their kisses, but that was where the similarities ended.

Determined not to be a prisoner of her past mistakes

any longer, Brooke shifted in her chair and let her cheek rest against Patrick's shoulder. He turned his head and touched his lips to her temple, and she felt herself teetering precariously on the edge of something scary and unknown.

Maybe she was walking a dangerous path, but with Patrick at her side, she couldn't help but want to take the next step.

"That was *totally awesome*," Brendan declared, as they were exiting the theater. "What did you think, Mr. Patrick?"

"I think you're right," he agreed.

"Mom?" Brendan prompted.

"Totally awesome," she echoed.

But her tone lacked the enthusiasm of her words, making Patrick suspect that something was bothering her. And he thought he had an idea what it might be.

For more than seven years, Brooke had been a single mom. During that time, it had been just her and Brendan—and her parents, but Sandra and Bruce Langley had defined roles in their grandson's life. Patrick was a new factor in the equation, and it was going to take some time to balance things out.

Until then, he suspected there would be a lot of one steps forward and two steps back, because Brooke was going to need some time to get used to sharing her son's attention and affection.

Though he was parked on the opposite side of the parking lot, Patrick walked with Brooke and Brendan to her truck.

"Thanks, Mom," Brendan said, as she buckled him into his booster seat. "I had a great 'versary tonight."

She kissed the tip of his nose. "You're welcome."

"I had a great time, too," Patrick said, when she'd closed Brendan's door.

She managed a weary smile. "Good night, Patrick."

"That's it?" he asked. "You're not going to invite me to come over for a cup of coffee?"

"It's late."

"It's not that late. And I'm wired from all the sugar I had during the movie."

"That's what happens when you add gummy bears and Milk Duds to your popcorn," she said.

"But it was good, wasn't it?"

"It was…interesting," she said, her tone softening a little.

"Coffee?" he prompted again.

She sighed. "One cup."

He followed her home and pulled into the driveway behind her. As he got out of his truck, she was opening the back door of her vehicle.

"What are you doing?" he asked, as she started to lift her son.

"He's asleep," she said in a whisper.

"I can see that. But you can't be planning to carry him up all those stairs," he said incredulously.

"I do it all the time," she told him.

"Not tonight," Patrick said. "I'll take him."

"I can manage," she protested, then huffed out a breath as he easily lifted the slumbering child into his arms.

"You might want to go ahead and unlock the door," he suggested.

So she did, and turned on the hall light so Patrick could find his way to the boy's bedroom, where she folded back the covers on her son's bed.

Patrick gently laid Brendan down on the mattress, then stood back as Brooke removed his coat and boots, pulled up the covers and kissed his forehead. The effortlessness of the routine confirmed that it was indeed something she did all the time, and reminded him that, despite his growing feelings for the single mom and her son, they shared a bond that he couldn't compete with or—thanks to his dysfunctional upbringing—even understand.

"Regular or decaf?" Brooke asked, as he followed her into the kitchen.

"Regular," he said, making an effort to shake off his melancholy.

She selected a pod from the basket beside the brewer and popped it into the machine.

"So what did Brendan mean when he said he had a great anniversary tonight?" he asked, as she passed the mug of coffee to him.

"Oh, we went out tonight because my parents were out celebrating their thirty-eighth anniversary."

"Thirty-eight years—that's impressive," he noted.

She nodded. "And even after all those years of marriage, and more than four decades together, they still enjoy hanging out," she said, sounding just a little bit wistful.

"You want the same thing," he realized.

"Someday," she agreed.

He wondered why the admission didn't make him panic. Of course, "someday" suggested a future event, and she'd given no indication that she was thinking about a future with *him*. Heck, she'd even hesitated before inviting him to a two-and-a-half-hour movie.

"You were lucky to live with their example," he said. "My parents wouldn't inspire anyone to matrimony. More than once, I've heard my mom remark that she only ever planned to have two kids—Jenna only happened because she and my dad were more focused on their reconciliation than birth control.

"Considering how many times my parents separated and got back together over the years, I'd probably have a dozen more siblings except my dad had a vasectomy before Jenna was born."

"But your parents are still together?" she asked.

"They're together *again*," he said. "They were married for sixteen years. Then they divorced and lived apart for nine years. During that time, they each had several other relationships before reconciling and remarrying ten years ago."

"Still, it must say something about their feelings for one another that they found their way back together," she ventured.

"Maybe," he said, sounding dubious. But then his thoughts moved on to something else, and he smiled. "Their anniversary is in the fall, and my mom wanted a big celebration this past year. Somehow she convinced Jenna to plan the party—or maybe Jenna volunteered." He shrugged. "Either way, my parents gave her the guest list and told her what they wanted in the way of food and drink, and left Jenna in charge of the rest."

"What went wrong?" Brooke asked.

"That depends on who tells the story," he said. "From Jenna's perspective, everything went according to plan. From my parents' perspective, she ruined their thirty-fifth anniversary.

"Because they were expecting a thirty-fifth anniversary party, counting from their first wedding, but all the banners and balloons and table decorations Jenna ordered had the number ten on them, which was the actual number of years since their second marriage. As much as our parents might want to pretend that they've been happy together since the beginning, the rest of us haven't forgotten the nasty fights inevitably followed by days—or sometimes weeks—of icy silence."

"Note to self—don't ever mess with Jenna Stafford," Brooke remarked.

He grinned. "Nobody ever does more than once."

Though he was tempted to linger, he swallowed the last mouthful of the one cup of coffee she'd promised him, set down the empty mug and stood up.

"I really did have a good time with you and Brendan tonight," he told her.

"I did, too," she said, walking him to the door.

"So…can I call you sometime?"

That earned him a smile. "Absolutely."

"Good."

"You can even kiss me good-night, if you want."

So he kissed her good-night.

And it was a really long, really great kiss, after which

he drove back to the ranch with his window down in a futile effort to cool the heat in his blood.

There, finally, was the sign Melissa had been looking for.

Not a figurative signal from the universe, but an actual painted-on-wood, secured-in-the-ground sign announcing Silver Star Vacation Ranch.

She turned into the long drive, grateful and relieved to know that she'd arrived. And after more than twelve hours on the road, she was eager to park her car and stretch her legs.

Or maybe stretch her whole body, preferably on a soft bed.

"I didn't think you were going to be here until tomorrow," Patrick said, opening his arms to her.

Though she hadn't seen her cousin in almost two years, he hadn't changed a bit. Well, except for the fact that he'd traded his designer suits for cowboy boots. But when his familiar arms wrapped around her, she felt the unexpected sting of tears behind her eyes as she hugged him back, grateful for his warmth and his strength and especially his welcome.

"I decided to drive right through," she told him.

"That's a long drive," he remarked, a hint of concern in his voice.

"I was eager to get here."

"Well, welcome to the Silver Star," he said, spreading his arms wide to encompass the land and buildings around him.

She turned in a slow circle to survey every direction.

"Toto, I have a feeling we're not in Seattle anymore," she murmured, paraphrasing Dorothy.

"There's no yellow brick road, but that flagstone path leads to the house and a fresh pot of coffee."

"That sounds great," she said, popping the trunk of her car. "Let me just grab my bags and—"

"I've got 'em," he said, effortlessly lifting them out.

"Not that I don't appreciate the help, but aren't I supposed to be working for you?"

He grinned. "I'll show you around the ranch today and shackle you in the kitchen tomorrow."

"Seems fair," she said and followed him to the house.

"It's pretty isolated out here," he said, sounding almost apologetic. "Town isn't too far, but there's not a lot to do there, either."

"It's great," she said. "Really. I meant what I said about wanting a change."

She tried to sound positive and upbeat, but apparently she didn't quite succeed because Patrick's next question was "Anything you want to talk about?"

"Nope."

He held her gaze for a long moment, as if trying to decide if he should press for more details. But he finally shrugged, and she let out the breath she'd been holding.

"In that case, I'll show you to your room."

Chapter Fourteen

Since Brendan had discovered that Patrick had a dog—despite the rancher's repeated denials of ownership—he wanted to visit the Silver Star every day to play with Princess. Brooke frequently gave in to his requests because it gave her an excuse to see Patrick and occasionally sneak away with him to steal a few kisses. And while she was enjoying spending time with the rancher, she was careful to keep the nature of their relationship a secret from her son for fear that it would lead to expectations of the three of them becoming a family.

When they arrived at the ranch Thursday afternoon, Patrick wasn't anywhere to be found and Stormy was absent from the paddock, so she assumed he'd taken the animal out for some exercise. Princess was outside today, too, exploring in the sunshine. But as soon as

Brendan called to her, she came running—or waddling, considering the girth of her swollen belly.

Though Princess was moving more slowly these days, she still loved playing catch or tug-of-war, but she seemed just as happy snuggling up with Brendan and would let him pet her for hours. And it seemed like hours had passed when a pretty brunette with deep green eyes came out of the house and asked, "Does anybody here like peanut butter cookies?"

Brendan's hand shot up in the air. "I do!"

"That's lucky," she said. "Because I just took a tray out of the oven and I don't want to eat them all by myself."

"You must be Melissa," Brooke said.

"And you're Brooke," she said, shaking the proffered hand.

"And I'm Brendan," he chimed in.

"I would have guessed that, if you'd given me a chance," Melissa said, with an indulgent smile.

"I'm impatient," he said.

The cook chuckled at that. "So what do you say to cookies and milk, Brendan the Impatient?"

"Can I say 'yes,' Mom?" he asked hopefully.

"You can say 'yes, please,'" she told him. "But make sure you wash your hands."

"I will," he promised. Then to Melissa he said, "Yes, please."

"I've got coffee, too," Patrick's cousin said to Brooke. "If that's your preference."

"I'd love a cup," Brooke said. "Just let me give Princess a quick check first."

She didn't think she stayed with the dog for very long after Brendan had gone inside with Melissa, but by the time she made it to the house, there was nothing left of the cookies but a few crumbs and her son was in the family room watching TV.

"So when did you get into town?" Brooke asked Melissa, as she sat at the island with her mug of coffee.

"Three days ago, and I'm leaving tomorrow for a three-day culinary expo in Vegas."

"So culture shock hasn't set in yet?"

Melissa smiled as she shook her head. "I know it's going to be an adjustment, but I think I'm going to like it. Especially with Jenna living here, too."

"Does Patrick know she's living here?" Brooke wondered.

Melissa grinned. "She thinks he might, but so far, he hasn't said anything about it."

Then the door opened and Patrick came in, stomping snow off his boots.

"Actually, I just remembered that I've got something I have to do," Melissa said, and with a quick wave she was gone.

"That was weird," Brooke said.

"What was?" Patrick asked, glancing around to ensure they were alone before bending down to press a quick kiss to her lips.

She shook her head, deciding it didn't really matter why the other woman had made a hasty escape, because it meant that she could steal another of the rancher's delicious kisses.

Patrick looked pointedly at the empty plate as he

poured himself a mug of coffee. "Did I miss out on cookies?"

Brooke nodded. "Freshly baked peanut butter," she said. "I didn't get any, either, because by the time I came in, they were gone."

"Melissa knows her way around the kitchen," Patrick said.

"That's why you hired her, isn't it?"

"Of course," he admitted.

"So why does it sound as if you're second-guessing your decision?" Brooke prompted.

"Because I can't shake the feeling that there's something going on with her that she's not telling me."

"If there is, it might be because it's none of your business," she pointed out gently.

"I bet she'll tell Sarah," he mused. "No one can keep a secret from Sarah."

Brooke shook her head. "Are you even listening to me?"

"Of course I'm listening. But she's my cousin, and if—"

"No," she interjected. "I mean, I know she's your cousin, and that makes the lines a little blurry, but she's here to cook for your guests."

And though the ranch wasn't yet officially open for business, within days of the website going live, he'd received dozens of inquiries and even a handful of bookings for the weekend of his grand opening.

"Would you be prying into the details of her life if she was a stranger you'd hired?" Brooke asked, returning to her original point.

"No," he admitted.

"Then let it be," she advised.

"Okay," he said. "I'll let it be *if* you take a walk out to the barn with me so we can make out in the tack room."

She lifted a brow. "You seem to be under the illusion that you're negotiating from a position of power here, when it really doesn't matter all that much to me whether you let it go or you don't."

"Does that mean you won't take a walk with me?" he asked, sounding disappointed.

"No, I'll take the walk," she said. "But only because I really want to make out with you."

He grinned. "That's a good enough reason for me."

Brooke was taking a short break between appointments at the clinic the next day when Larissa handed her a stack of messages. While there didn't seem to be anything urgent, she noticed that Patrick had called three times, so she picked up the phone and dialed his number.

"I think Princess is in labor. What should I do?" he asked, sounding like an adorably flustered expectant father.

"You've already done everything you can to help her," Brooke reminded him. "She's comfortable in the whelping box, and she's got a heat lamp to keep her warm. The rest is up to her."

"There's nothing else?"

"Keep me posted," she said.

After that, she put Princess out of her mind while she

dealt with other patients—at least until Patrick called again two hours later.

"Any puppies yet?" Brooke asked him.

"No. And she seems absolutely miserable. I know I'm probably overreacting," he admitted, "but is there any chance you can come out to check on her?"

"I really can't," Brooke said apologetically. "I've still got three patients in the waiting room. But if you're concerned, you can bring her into the clinic."

He was there in less than thirty minutes.

"You must have left the ranch as soon as I hung up the phone," Brooke remarked, as she entered the exam room where he waited with Princess.

"Pretty much," he agreed.

She gently stroked the dog's swollen belly. "How are you doing, Princess?"

The dog looked at her with pleading eyes, a low whine sounding deep in her throat.

"You're having a rough go of it, are you?" She kept her hands in place as the animal's belly tightened with a contraction. "Yeah, I've been there," she murmured soothingly. "Giving birth can be a scary process, but you're not alone."

Princess's tail thumped against the table, making Brooke smile.

Then she saw the bloody discharge.

Patrick paced the waiting room, waiting and hating every minute of it. When Brooke had told him that a cesarean would give her the best chance to save Princess and her pups, he'd immediately consented to the surgery. But now that he was on the other side of the wall, her words echoing in his head, he was forced to accept that "best chance" meant there was still a chance the dog could lose her pups—and that he could lose Princess.

He hadn't chosen the dog, but she'd apparently chosen him. In the beginning she might only have been looking for a warm, dry place to sleep, but over the past several weeks she'd been his constant companion. Except when Brendan was at the Silver Star—then Princess readily abandoned Patrick in favor of the boy's attention and affection.

He didn't mind. In fact, he enjoyed watching them together. There was something both simple and sweet about the bond between the child and the dog. And if he was being completely honest, Princess wasn't the only one who looked forward to Brendan's visits to the ranch. Patrick was growing attached to the boy, too.

And Brendan's mother, who was scrubbing up to perform emergency surgery on Princess, bringing Patrick's thoughts full circle again. Weary and worried, he dropped into one of the hard plastic chairs just as the bell chimed over the door.

"Hey, Mr. Patrick!" Brendan said, as he crossed the room to stand in front of him. "Gramma dropped me off 'cause she had to go to a 'pointment and Mom said we could get pizza for dinner when she's done work," he explained. "What are you doing here?"

"Your mom's helping Princess have her babies."

"Cool." Brendan sat down beside him. "Have you been waiting very long?"

Forever.

Patrick glanced at his watch. "Half an hour."

"A lot of people think that it's easy for animals to have babies," Brendan said, perhaps trying to reassure him. "But sometimes they need help."

He nodded.

"And sometimes a mom doesn't survive having babies," the boy continued. "And sometimes the babies don't survive being born. Then there are creatures—like spiders—that actually eat their own babies." He made a face, then hastened to assure Patrick, "But you don't have to worry about Princess. Dogs don't do that."

"Good to know," Patrick said, both impressed and a little unnerved by the child's matter-of-fact accounting of the harsh realities of nature. Because the last thing he wanted to think about right now was the possibility that he might lose Princess or any of her pups.

And what if it was his fault?

What if he'd waited too long to bring Princess to the clinic?

"Do you wanna play cards while we're waiting?" Brendan asked, as if aware that Patrick was in desperate need of a distraction.

"Do you have any cards?" he asked.

"No, but Larissa keeps some in her desk," Brendan said, heading to the counter to talk to the receptionist.

Sure enough, he returned a few minutes later with a deck of cards in hand.

"Crazy Eights or Go Fish?" he asked.

"Crazy Eights," Patrick decided. "But you'll have to remind me how it's played."

It turned out the kid was pretty good at Crazy Eights. In fact, Brendan won five straight games.

"You suck at this," he said. "Maybe we should try Go Fish."

But Patrick sucked at that, too, and Brendan won several rounds before he gathered the cards up and stuffed them back in the box.

"Are you worried about Princess?" the boy asked.

"A little," he admitted.

"You don't have to worry. My mom will take real good care of her."

Then Brendan put his hand on Patrick's, as if to offer comfort.

And looking at the child's small fingers curled around his much larger hand, he was comforted—and grateful not to be alone.

To Brooke, there was no greater joy than the miracle of new life. Whether it was the hatching of an egg, the foaling of a horse or the birth of a human baby. Each and every time, it was beautiful and amazing. Sure, it could be messy and complicated, but in the end, when there was new life, it was all worthwhile.

Today, it had been very worthwhile.

Stripping off her gloves and gown, she went out to the waiting area to share the good news.

Brendan saw her first and immediately bounced up from his chair and raced over. "Did you help Princess have her puppies? Can I see them?"

"Let me talk to Mr. Patrick first," she said, as the rancher rose slowly from his chair, worry etched in the tiny lines beside his eyes and in the set of his jaw. "Princess is his dog."

Of course, Brendan stayed right by her side, determined to hear all the details.

"Congratulations," she said to the rancher and watched the weight of worry visibly lift from his shoulders.

"They made it?"

She nodded, smiling. "They made it. Three boys and three girls."

"How's Princess?"

"Right now she's still a little groggy from the sedation, but she's already showing an interest in her babies. I'd suggest giving her another half hour before you take them home."

"Take them home?" he echoed, sounding panicked. "Wouldn't it be better if they stayed here?"

She chuckled softly. "No, it would be better for mom, and her babies, to be in familiar surroundings."

"But—I don't have the first clue what to do with them."

"I could help," Brendan was quick to offer. "I know a lot about puppies."

"You're hired," Patrick immediately replied.

"Except that child labor laws—and this mom—prohibit working on school nights," Brooke said.

Brendan pouted. "But I wanna see the puppies."

"You can go back and see the puppies in a few minutes," she promised.

"I really don't know what to do with them when I get them home," Patrick said to Brooke.

"Just put them in the whelping box and make sure Princess has access to food and water. She'll take care of her puppies."

He did as Brooke had instructed, and then he stood there for a long while, watching them and feeling helpless. The puppies were so tiny and Princess so wiped out from the unsuccessful labor followed by the surgery that he didn't want to leave them alone in the barn overnight. Thankfully there was a cot in the tack room.

But the next morning, he wasn't feeling so thankful.

Because while the narrow bed might have been okay for a short nap—or a short child—it wasn't built for the overnight comfort of a full-grown man. After six hours on that narrow bed, Patrick didn't feel any more rested than when he'd first lain down on it, and his bones creaked and groaned in protest when he stood up.

He made a quick trip to the house to take a hot shower and brush his teeth before returning to the barn. Glancing at the bowl of dog food, he thought Princess might have eaten a few bites. He was sure she'd at least drunk some of the water.

The puppies were clearly hungry now, too, rooting around in search of their breakfast. Though their eyes were still closed, they didn't seem to have any difficulty finding the source of their sustenance, and they suckled hungrily. Patrick winced in sympathy with Princess as the tiny mouths tugged and pulled on their mother's nipples, though she didn't seem at all bothered by their feeding.

Clearly Brooke had been right—the new mama had

everything under control and would have been just fine if he'd spent the night in his own bed.

Never again, he promised his aching muscles.

He didn't realize he'd spoken aloud until an amused female voice asked, "Never again what?"

"Never again am I pretending to sleep on that cot," he admitted to Brooke.

"You spent the night out here," she said.

It wasn't a question, but he nodded anyway.

"Maybe this will help."

She handed him a foil-wrapped—

"Breakfast burrito."

"What did I do to deserve this?" he wondered, eagerly unwrapping it.

"You spent the night pretending to sleep on a cot so that you could keep an eye on your dog and her babies."

"She's not—" He sighed. "Damn, she is my dog, isn't she?"

"Without a doubt," Brooke said.

He bit into the burrito. "Mmm," he said, around a mouthful of egg and cheese. And then, "But how did you guess I'd spend the night out here?"

"I'm a vet, and I know things." She smiled then. "I also remembered Melissa mentioning that she'd be away at a culinary expo this week, so I guessed you wouldn't get a hot breakfast and probably wouldn't leave Princess long enough to even pour a bowl of cereal."

"I would have. Eventually," he said. "But this is better."

"Breakfast burritos are a favorite of Brendan's, so I made one for him and one for you, and that gave me an excuse to come out and take another peek at the puppies."

"Just the puppies?"

She shrugged. "Maybe I didn't think it would be so bad to see you, too."

He popped the last bite into his mouth. "Did I tell you how amazing you were yesterday?"

"I'm flattered you think so," she said.

"You saved Princess and her puppies."

"I only did what any vet would have done."

"Maybe," he acknowledged. "But I've never known another vet to make competent performance of duties look so sexy."

"Yeah, I've been told scrubs are a good look for me," she said dryly.

"You look good in anything," he assured her. Then he winked. "And even better in nothing."

"That's my cue to head out," she decided.

"Busy day today?"

"Always."

"Well, thank you again for breakfast."

"You're welcome." She lifted a hand to his cheek, rubbed her palm against the raspy stubble, then dropped her arm and stepped back. "You should try and get some sleep."

He caught her wrist and drew her close again, dipping his head to touch his mouth to hers. "I'd go to bed right now if you'd go with me."

She shook her head. "You know I can't."

"But are you at least a little bit tempted?"

"More than a little," she admitted.

"It's not much of a consolation, but I'll take it," he said. And he took another kiss for good measure, too.

Brooke continued on her way to Rolling Meadows, but instead of thinking of the day ahead, she found herself thinking about Patrick. And not just the kiss—though her lips were still tingling from the brief but potent brush of his lips—but his obvious attachment to the dog he'd foolishly tried to deny was his. This even after he'd paced the floor of the reception area while Princess was in surgery, paid the bill for the procedure and stayed up with her through the night to look after her while she looked after her babies.

For all his claims about not being ready to be a father, he had impressive paternal instincts. And though she knew it was crazy, she couldn't help but feel a little envious of the canine mom.

When she'd given birth to Brendan, she hadn't had a partner to share the joy and excitement of the moment. Yes, she'd been fortunate to have her mother as her birthing coach and her father in the waiting room. But it wasn't the same as having a partner to share all the exciting and terrifying moments along the way.

And though she'd told herself she didn't need a man to hold her hand, there were times when it would have been nice not to be alone. Such as when she'd heard her baby's heartbeat for the first time; when she'd seen the grainy image on the ultrasound monitor; when she'd felt him move inside her the first time, a gentle flutter, or, five months later, an impatient kick. And especially when her water broke in the middle of the night.

She sometimes wondered what it would be like to share those special moments with someone—and the wondering inevitably led to yearning. Not just because she really did hope to give Brendan a brother or sister someday, but because she wanted a partner to share all the trials and triumphs of parenthood and of life, someone to grow old with, someone she could always count on.

But Patrick wasn't that person. Just because he was doting on his dog and half a dozen adorable puppies didn't mean he was ready to make a personal commitment. And based on what he'd told her about his parents' relationship, she could understand why he wasn't looking for a happily-ever-after.

Still, it made her sad that he didn't believe happy endings were possible. And it made her wonder if anything—or anyone—might ever be able to change his mind.

Chapter Fifteen

"Something smells good," Patrick said, sniffing the air as he walked into the kitchen the day after Melissa's return.

"It's Grandma Stafford's chili recipe," she said. "With an extra dash of Tabasco and a few chili peppers."

"When can we eat? I'm starving."

"You wouldn't be starving if you'd come in for lunch," she pointed out.

"I was out with Dean, marking the riding trails."

"Well, I'm starving, too," she confided. "So have a seat and I'll dish this up."

He sat, and she served him a bowl of piping hot chili topped with shredded cheese and a sprinkling of green onions.

He dug into the meal with enthusiasm.

"This is really good," he told her. "A little spicy, but good."

"I can dial back the heat for your guests, if you think it's too much."

He nodded. "I have to admit, when I saw the menu from your restaurant in Seattle, I was a little worried that you were going to make stuff with edible flowers and fancy sauces that weekend cowboys weren't going to want to eat."

"I can do edible flowers and fancy sauces, but I understand comfort food, too," she assured him.

"I'm convinced," he said, dipping his spoon into his bowl again.

And though Melissa had claimed she was starving only a few minutes earlier, she abruptly pushed her bowl away and reached for her water.

As she lifted the glass to her lips, Patrick noticed that her hand wasn't quite steady and her face was suddenly pale.

"Are you okay?" he asked, concerned.

She sipped her water, then nodded as she set the glass down again.

"Are you sure? You look—"

She shoved her stool away from the island and bolted to the bathroom. Only a few seconds later, he heard the unmistakable sound of retching.

He pushed his own bowl away with the fleeting thought that he might have to reconsider their professional association if she'd given him food poisoning. But his speculation was quickly supplanted by concern for his cousin. Should he take her a glass of water? Get her a cool cloth for her face?

He was still debating whether to give her privacy or offer assistance when he heard the toilet flush, then the tap run. A moment later, she returned to the kitchen.

"Sorry about that," she said, sounding both embarrassed and remorseful. "I didn't mean to put a damper on your appetite."

"Yeah, I think I'll make a sandwich," he said, though his appetite had definitely been dampened.

"There's nothing wrong with the chili," she insisted indignantly.

He lifted his brows. "Then why were you puking your guts out?"

"Because apparently my morning sickness prefers to make an appearance during the latter part of the day."

Patrick stared at her, as if he didn't quite understand what Melissa was saying. Apparently some people couldn't even recognize a sign when they were hit over the head with it—a thought that might have made her smile at another time. But she didn't feel much like smiling now.

"I'm pregnant," she said bluntly.

"But…" he sputtered, clearly taken aback by her announcement. "You didn't say anything about being pregnant when you offered to take the job."

"Because being pregnant won't interfere with my ability to do the job."

"Of course it will," he said. "Because a pregnancy leads to a baby."

She opened her eyes wide, feigning surprise. "Is that how it works?"

He scowled, clearly not appreciating her sarcasm. "And a baby is a big responsibility."

It was his tone more than his words that made her understand the cause of his panic. "You don't have to worry, Patrick. My baby won't be *your* responsibility."

"Except that you and your baby will be living here, won't you?" And then his gaze narrowed as another thought occurred to him. "That's why you were so eager to get away from Seattle."

"One of the reasons," she acknowledged. But she refused to feel guilty about her deception and she wasn't going to apologize for doing what she needed to do.

"Does the father know about the baby?" he asked.

"Of course," she said.

"Your parents?"

"Not yet." And maybe she did feel a little guilty about that, but Melissa needed some time to decide what she wanted to do before she shared the news.

"So I'm harboring a fugitive," he concluded.

"They know I'm here," she said. "They just don't know that they're going to be grandparents in less than seven months."

"You have to tell them, Melissa."

"I know. I just need to figure some things out first." Such as how to convince her parents that she was capable of raising a child on her own without their support or interference, and that wouldn't happen until she'd managed to convince herself.

"Anything I can help with?" he asked.

She smiled at that and gave him a quick hug. "You already have. You gave me a job and a place to live."

"I'm still going to have to hire someone else," he realized.

"What? No," she protested.

"I don't mean to replace you, but to help you," he hastened to clarify.

"Maybe just for a few weeks, before and after the baby is born," she said.

"Whatever you need," he told her.

And her eyes filled with grateful tears.

By the time Brooke finished at the clinic, she was exhausted. It hadn't just been a long day but a difficult one, as she'd had to break the news that Marmalade, Peggy Bartlett's beloved feline companion of seventeen years, had tested positive for lymphoma—again.

Two years earlier, the orange tabby had successfully undergone chemotherapy treatments and gained a new lease on life. When the cat was first diagnosed, only six months after Peggy had buried her husband, the woman was determined to do everything she could to keep the cat alive—so that she wouldn't lose someone else she loved. Brooke had completely understood and supported her choice, though Peggy was still making monthly payments to the clinic for those treatments.

This time, the woman made the difficult decision to end Marmalade's suffering. As Brooke administered the injection—every vet's least favorite part of the job—she cried right along with Peggy. Thankfully, Marmalade was her last patient of the day, so she was able to take some time to sit with the older woman and offer condolences that she knew didn't make anyone feel any better.

When she finally left the clinic, she wanted only to go home, put her feet up and watch something mindless on TV. But of course she couldn't, because she'd promised Brendan that she'd take him to the Silver Star to see Princess and her puppies.

"Have you named the puppies yet?"

It was the first question Brendan asked Patrick upon their arrival at the ranch.

"No," he said. "I thought I should let their new owners give them names."

"You've found homes for them already?" Brooke asked.

"I've had a couple phone calls, thanks to the notice you put up at the clinic, but I haven't met any prospective owners yet or made any promises."

"You should at least keep one," Brendan said. "Princess might be sad and lonely if she has to give up all her babies."

"I wasn't even planning to keep Princess," Patrick reminded him.

Brooke smiled at that. "And now she's wearing a collar with her name and your phone number on it."

"A collar *you* bought for her," he reminded her.

"You put it on her."

"You should keep Leia," Brendan suggested.

"Who's Leia?" Patrick asked warily.

"The one that looks most like Princess."

He sighed. "You've come up with names for all the puppies, haven't you?"

Brendan nodded. "The other girls are Rey and Rose," he said, pointing to each one in turn. "And the boys are Luke, Han and Finn."

"It's possible the new owners won't be *Star Wars* fans, you know," Patrick told him.

The boy frowned, as if he couldn't imagine such a possibility. "But they might let them keep the names anyway."

"They might," he agreed, before turning his attention to Brooke. "Everything okay? You got quiet all of a sudden."

"Just a really long day," she said.

"Anything you want to talk about?"

She glanced in Brendan's direction. Though her son seemed preoccupied with the puppies, he had an uncanny knack for absorbing every word of a conversation not intended for his ears. So while it might have been nice to share the details of her crappy day with Patrick and lean into the strength of his embrace, she only shook her head.

Understanding, he didn't push for details. Instead he asked, "Anything I can do to help?"

Though she appreciated the offer, she shook her head again.

He wrapped his arms around her anyway and held her close for a long moment, and it helped a lot.

Friday night, Patrick picked up takeout from Diggers' and took it to Brooke's apartment to share with her and Brendan. He'd wanted to take them out to the restaurant, but Brooke preferred to dine in. She claimed she was wiped out after a long week at work, and while that was probably true, he suspected it was more true that she wasn't ready to make a public statement about their relationship. Or even a private statement, as evidenced by her determination to keep Brendan in the dark.

"Melissa told me her news," she said, after Brendan had gone to bed and they could talk more freely.

"So you know I wasn't wrong when I suspected that she was holding something back," he said.

"She's still qualified for the job."

"Overqualified," he admitted. "And she deliberately manipulated me into giving her the job."

"You wanted a cook. She wanted a job. That sounds more like a mutually beneficial arrangement than manipulation to me," Brooke remarked.

"She wanted out of Seattle and jumped at the first opportunity that presented itself."

"Maybe she did need a place to go and some distance from the father of her child," she allowed.

He frowned at that. "What do you know that I don't? Did the father threaten her in some way? Did he—"

She held up a hand to halt his tirade. "I don't know the details of her situation, but I know he made it clear that if she insisted on having the baby, she was on her own."

"Apparently I need to go to Seattle and kick someone's worthless—"

"No, you don't," she said, cutting him off again. "What you need to do is trust Melissa to make her own choices."

"Because clearly that's worked out for her so far," he said dryly.

"Maybe a pregnancy isn't something she would have chosen at this time in her life," Brooke acknowledged coolly. "But it might turn out that this baby is the best thing that could have happened to her."

"I'm sorry. I wasn't thinking about the fact that…" He trailed off, as if uncertain how to finish the thought.

"That eight years ago, I was in the same position your cousin is in right now?" she finished for him.

"Yeah," he admitted.

"But I had my parents to support me. Melissa came here because she doesn't believe hers will. And because she trusts you." She pinned him with her gaze. "Don't disappoint her."

"Is that what you're waiting for?" he wondered. "Me to disappoint you?"

"I thought we were talking about your cousin."

"And now we're talking about us," he said. "Or maybe about the fact that you don't want anyone to know that there even is an 'us.'"

"That's not true," she denied. "There are plenty of people who know."

"If 'plenty' translates to 'a select few who won't slip up and say something in front of Brendan,'" he remarked dryly.

"I'm not going to apologize for wanting to protect my son from gossip."

"Is that all you're protecting him from?" Patrick challenged.

"History teaches a hard lesson," she said. "And I don't want to be the fool who didn't learn from her mistakes."

"I hope you're not comparing me to your ex, because I would never have let a woman I'd been involved with raise our child alone."

"Let me guess… You would have offered to marry her."

"Of course," he immediately replied.

"Well, for your information, Xander did offer to marry me. And I said yes, because I was twenty-two years old and terrified by the idea of having a baby on my own."

He was clearly taken aback by this revelation. "You were married to Brendan's father?"

"No. I wasn't foolish enough to go through with it after I found him in bed with my roommate," she confided reluctantly. Because eight years later, she was still embarrassed to admit that she'd fallen for a guy who'd obviously thought so little of her.

"He didn't even apologize," she continued. "That's when I realized he'd wanted to get caught. That he probably chose her so he would get caught, so I wouldn't marry him."

"He was an asshole." Patrick's blunt response soothed some of the residual sting from Xander's cruel actions.

"He was," she agreed readily.

He frowned. "And you think I'm like him?"

"No, I don't think you're anything like him," she said.

"Then what's the problem?" he asked.

"The problem is that I don't really trust my own judgment anymore," she admitted. "And it's not only my heart I have to worry about this time."

Now that he knew a little bit more about Brooke's situation with her ex, in addition to the previous history she'd shared, Patrick wasn't surprised that she had trust issues. And while he wished she would show a little more faith in him, he wasn't entirely sure he deserved it.

He would never cheat on her—or any woman, but he'd never been able to make a commitment to a woman, either. The closest he'd ever come was shopping for an engagement ring. But he'd held off buying one in favor of taking Kari to the store so that she could pick out what she wanted. It turned out to be a good call, because she hadn't wanted to plan a future with him.

Unhappy with the trek down memory lane, Patrick was grateful to be distracted by his grandfather's arrival at the ranch.

"You're a long way from Crooked Creek," he remarked, greeting him with a hug.

"I'm on my way to Helen's for dinner," Gramps said, referring to the woman that he'd been dating for more than two years now.

It had been a surprise to the whole family to discover that Jesse Blake had opened up his heart again after mourning the loss of his wife so deeply and for so long. But in one of those odd twists of fate, Gramps had met his lady friend at a birthday party for Spencer's daughter, Dani.

And while it was strange for Patrick to see his grandfather flirting and cuddling with a woman who wasn't his grandmother—or really, any woman at his age—Sarah was right. There was a definite spring in the old guy's step since he'd started spending time with Helen.

"And since I was passing by, I thought I'd stop by to see the pups Dani's been talking about." Gramps continued his explanation.

"They're pretty darn adorable," Patrick told him, leading the way to the barn.

"Are you planning on keeping any?" his grandfather asked.

"I wasn't even planning on keeping Princess," Patrick confided. "But somehow she's wearing a pink collar with my contact information on the tag."

"Princess?" Gramps echoed, sounding amused.

He shrugged, unwilling to admit it was the vet's son who'd named the dog—or that Brendan's attachment to the animal had undoubtedly been a factor in Patrick's decision to keep her.

"Well, every ranch should have a dog," his grandfather said, surveying the area where the canine mama was in residence with her pups. "So maybe it's lucky that she found you."

"I would have preferred to be found by a shepherd or Lab mix."

"A labradoodle is part Lab," Gramps pointed out.

"And part fluff ball."

"Which might explain why the puppies are so darn adorable." His grandfather's usually stern expression softened as he watched the little ones snuggle close to their mama.

"If you believe every ranch should have a dog, is that

why you're here?" Patrick asked, picking up the thread of their earlier conversation. "Do you want to take one of the pups home to Crooked Creek?"

"I'm thinking about it," Gramps said.

"Have you talked to Spencer and Kenzie about this?"

"Why would I? I don't need their permission to get a dog just because we all live at Crooked Creek."

"You do if you plan on giving that dog to Dani," Patrick said.

"I thought you'd be anxious to get rid of the pups, not try to talk potential adopters out of taking one off your hands."

"I want to see them go to good homes," he acknowledged. "I don't want them to be the cause of friction in a good home, and Spencer and Kenzie have their hands full enough right now with an almost seven-year-old and a new baby."

"Sounds like you might know something about the demands of a seven-year-old," his grandfather mused thoughtfully. "Makes me think there might be some truth to the rumors I've heard about you hanging out with the pretty vet and her son."

"It sounds to me like you didn't come here to see the puppies as much as to go on a fishing expedition."

As if to prove him wrong, Gramps shifted his attention back to the puppies. "Do they have names?"

"Apparently they do," Patrick said.

"Who's that one, with the lighter-colored fur?"

"Luke."

"Strange name for a dog," Gramps said.

Patrick just shrugged.

"Has anyone else asked about him?"

"Not specifically."

"Then you can reserve him for me."

Chapter Sixteen

"Five minutes," Brooke said, giving her son the usual warning so that he'd be ready and waiting when the school bus pulled up at the end of their driveway. "Did you brush your teeth?"

Brendan nodded and tugged his knit cap onto his head.

She slid his lunch box into the front pouch of his backpack and zipped it up.

He shoved his feet into his boots. "Can we go to the Silver Star after school today?"

Brooke shook her head. "Not today. I've got a full day at the clinic and then I've got to go check on Mr. Wallace's goats."

"You could drop me off at the Silver Star on your way," he said, as he fumbled with the zipper on his coat.

"No, I can't." She shook her head again as she helped him zip up. "But you can either come with me to see the goats or you can stay with Grandma."

Her son pouted. "Why can't I go to the Silver Star?"

"Because it's not on my way, and because you weren't invited." She put on her own coat and boots to wait outside with him.

"Patrick said I could visit the ranch anytime," he pointed out.

"Any time when you're with me," she acknowledged, wondering when her son had dropped the *Mister* and how that detail had escaped her notice until now. "He didn't offer to babysit you."

"I'm not a baby," Brendan said, slinging his backpack over his shoulder.

"No, you're not," she agreed. "But you're also not old enough to be left on your own, and Mr. Patrick might have other plans."

"But I want to help with the puppies."

"And that's a nice idea," Brooke said, as she steered him out the door. "But you wanting to help with the puppies would require me to drive fifteen miles out of my way and I don't have time for that today."

"I want to help with the puppies," he insisted, adopting the mutinous tone she knew only too well.

"And I told you not today," she reminded him, maintaining a level tone.

He folded his arms across his chest. "You're not the boss of me."

"Actually, being your mom pretty much means that

I *am* the boss of you," she said, giving up on any effort to de-escalate the situation.

"I wish I had a dad," Brendan shot back. "I bet a dad would let me go to the ranch."

She might have been less shocked if he'd slapped her, because his words stung more than a physical blow. And while her mind understood that he was lashing out because he wasn't getting his way, the heart that had only ever wanted what was best for her little boy was bruised and aching.

But there was nothing to be gained from letting him know how much his words had hurt her, so she drew in a slow, steadying breath and tried to respond calmly and rationally.

"Well, you've got me instead," she finally replied. "And I've already said you're not going today, so that's the end of the discussion. And if I hear one more word about the Silver Star or those puppies, you won't be going tomorrow, either."

"You're so mean!" Brendan protested, his eyes shiny with unshed tears.

She had no response to that, because she didn't doubt that, from his perspective, she was being mean. Because he couldn't possibly understand everything that she had to cram into a twenty-four-hour day. And in addition to all the usual duties and responsibilities, she was also trying to protect her little boy's heart.

Over the past couple of months, it had become apparent to Brooke that Brendan was growing far too attached to not just the ranch but the rancher. Patrick had been great with her son and genuinely seemed to enjoy hanging out with him, but what would happen when her relationship with Patrick ran its course? When he started dating someone else, would he still have time for Brendan? She wanted to believe that he would, but how could she expect Patrick to make her son a priority when the child's own father hadn't done so?

Of course, there was no way to explain any of this to a sensitive seven-year-old boy, so all she said was "There's your bus, honey."

She reached out to give him a quick hug, as she did every morning, but Brendan pulled away from her— for the first time ever—and made his way down the driveway.

The bus driver lifted his hand in greeting and Brooke waved back, managing a smile despite the heavy weight of her heart in her chest. Then she watched as Brendan made his way down the center aisle to take his usual seat by the window, but he kept his gaze focused forward instead of turning to wave, as he was accustomed to doing.

Brooke exhaled a weary sigh as the bus finally pulled away. With tears in her eyes, she turned toward her parents' house.

"Do you have coffee on?" she asked, walking into the kitchen after a perfunctory knock on the door.

"Always," her mom said.

Brooke sat at the table, wanting her mother's wise counsel more than another hit of caffeine.

Sandra poured two cups of coffee, and Brooke recapped the highlights of the conversation with her son as she sipped the hot drink.

"Did I overreact?" she wondered.

"Do you think you overreacted?"

"I don't know," she admitted. "I know he's excited about the puppies, but even before they were born, he was *always* asking to go to the Silver Star, so maybe I'm afraid that Patrick is the real draw, and—" emotion choked her voice "—I don't want Brendan to get hurt."

"Why are you so certain that he will?" Then, after a moment's hesitation, Sandra asked, "Or are you more worried that *you* will, Brooke?"

"I'm not certain," she admitted, wiping away a tear. "But Patrick told me at the beginning that he wasn't ready to be a father."

"And yet he's been spending an awful lot of time with you *and* your son over the past few weeks," her mom remarked. "He wouldn't be doing that if he didn't care about both of you."

Brooke sighed, because it was true. It was also true that she'd been holding back. Not because she didn't trust him, but because she was afraid to trust her own heart. A heart that was already more than halfway in love with him.

"Don't you think it's time to let go of the past and look to the future?" Sandra asked gently. "To take a chance and finally let yourself be happy?"

Maybe it was, she mused. "Being at the Silver Star certainly makes Brendan happy."

"And that's great, but what about you?" her mom prompted.

"I like being there, too," she confided. "Being with Patrick makes me happy. And gives me hope that the family I once dreamed of having might not be beyond my reach after all."

Sandra smiled, even as her eyes got misty. "Then give him a chance. Give *yourself* a chance."

Brooke decided that was good advice.

After hugging her mom and thanking her for the coffee, she headed toward the clinic. And she promised herself that the next time she saw Patrick, she would be honest about her feelings and her hopes for their future together.

Brooke felt so much better after talking to her mom that she managed to put the argument with Brendan out of her mind for most of the day. In fact, she even considered softening her stance and taking him to the Silver Star after dinner, but only if he didn't have any homework to do. Because how could she object to her son wanting to see Patrick when she wanted to see him, too?

Of course, that was before her dad walked into the exam room just as her four-legged patient walked out. Her quick smile immediately faded when she saw the expression on his face.

"What's wrong?"

Her father had never been one to tiptoe around bad news and he didn't do so now. "Brendan didn't get off the school bus today."

"What do you mean? Did Mom have to pick him up at school?" she asked, unable or unwilling to make sense of what he was saying.

"Your mom called the school, and the teacher on duty insisted she saw him in line for the bus. But when she called the bus company and they patched her through to the driver, he said Brendan never got on the bus."

"Then where is he?" Brooke demanded.

"Right now, no one seems to know."

Her father's words struck terror in her heart, and she had to grip the exam table with both hands for support.

"But we'll find him," Bruce promised.

"I know he was mad at me this morning," she admitted. "But I never thought he was the type of kid who would run away…" And then another, even more horrific, thought occurred to her. "But what if he didn't run away…? What if someone took him?"

"No one took him," Bruce said firmly, though he'd gone a little pale, obviously shaken by the thought.

"We should call the police," Brooke said.

"I already did. Sheriff Davidson was going to the school to talk to his teacher. And your mom's at home, because we thought someone should be there in case— *for when*—Brendan comes back."

Brooke nodded, needing to believe that her son would find his way home. Or that someone would find him. Until then, however, she had no idea where he was, and it terrified her to think of him wandering the streets alone.

"I've asked Larissa to reschedule the rest of your appointments so we can go out and start looking for Brendan right away. Your mom wanted to start organizing the neighbors into search parties, but the sheriff suggested we check out his favorite places around town first."

"Okay," she agreed, already making a mental list: the

playground by the school, Ridgemount Park, Jo's—for the video games. And then another possibility occurred to her. "The Silver Star."

"You think he'd head out to the ranch?" Bruce sounded dubious—and looked even more worried.

And Brooke understood why. The ranch was a nearly impossible distance from town on foot and the rural roads saw a fair amount of traffic traveling at highway speeds.

"I'll call Patrick." While she couldn't imagine that her son might have actually made his way out to the Silver Star, it was suddenly obvious to Brooke that the ranch was his ultimate destination.

"You can call from the car," her father said. "I'll drive."

Patrick was feeling pretty good about his life as he sat in front of his computer, double-checking reservation requests with room assignments for the grand opening of the Silver Star Vacation Ranch. With only a few weeks to go, everything was on track and on schedule. But the icing on the cake was his relationship with Brooke and Brendan. And, yeah, that had been a surprise to him, too. Not only that he would enter into a relationship with a single mom, but that he'd fall head over heels for her kid.

He wasn't ready to get down on one knee, but he wasn't freaked out by the idea that they might one day be a family, either. Okay, he was maybe a little freaked out—and worried about his ability to be a good husband and father, considering his own hadn't been much of a role model—but he wasn't completely freaked out. And that, he decided, was a definite step forward for him.

So when his phone rang and a quick glance at the screen identified Brooke as the caller, his lips curved automatically and he swiped to connect the call. "I was just think—"

"Brendan's missing."

Those two words not only stole his breath but his ability to form a coherent thought. "What—how—where—"

"I don't know," she said, interrupting him again. "But I think he might be on his way to the Silver Star."

He could hear the desperation and panic in her voice and the same emotions began to take root inside him. Questions continued to swirl in his mind, but he managed to keep them in his head this time, understanding that she didn't need him to add to her concerns.

"My dad and I are on our way there now," Brooke continued, "but if you could keep an eye out for him…"

"Of course," he immediately responded, pushing his chair away from the desk.

"Thanks."

Patrick heard the tremor in her voice and knew she was hanging on by a thread. He wanted to say something to reassure her, but he knew nothing would make her feel better until Brendan was found safe.

"I'll see you soon," he said instead.

Then he disconnected the call and shoved the phone into his back pocket. He felt as if there was a weight on his chest, making it difficult to draw air into his lungs.

"Patrick?"

He hadn't heard Melissa come into the room and he started now at the sound of her voice.

"Is something wrong?" she asked, sounding concerned.

He wasn't the type to panic. At least, he'd never been so before. But he was starting to feel panicky now as Brooke's words replayed in his head, an endless ominous loop. "Brendan's missing."

"Missing?" his cousin echoed. "Oh, no…the poor boy. And Brooke. She must be beside herself."

He nodded, because of course she was. Any parent would be frantic to discover that a child was missing, and he'd heard not just worry but fear for her son in Brooke's voice.

Patrick hadn't anticipated that he'd feel the same way. After all, he wasn't Brendan's father or stepfather—he wasn't even officially dating the boy's mother. He had absolutely no rights or responsibilities with respect to the child, and yet those words—*Brendan's missing*— had cut him off at the knees.

Because over the past couple of months, as he'd spent time with and got to know the little boy, he'd grown to care for him. A lot. And he couldn't bear to think of him lost or alone.

"What can I do to help?" Melissa asked now.

"I don't even know what I'm supposed to be doing," he confided, as he shoved his feet into his boots and reached for his coat. "But Brooke thinks Brendan might be on his way here."

"Here?" Worry etched a frown in Melissa's brow. "How would he find his way from town?"

"I don't know." Although there was a school bus that passed by every day, to pick up and drop off at the Carson place, just down the road. "But if Brendan's here, I'll find him."

"I'll put on a fresh pot of coffee."

He nodded and headed out the door.

Though he'd tried to sound confident when he'd said he'd find Brooke's son, he didn't expect it would be easy. Even if Brendan had known to get off the bus at the Carson residence, it was nearly a quarter mile from there to the Silver Star—assuming the kid knew east from west and didn't start walking in the wrong direction.

And apparently he did, because as soon as Patrick started down the driveway, he spotted a familiar pint-size figure in a blue ski jacket and red pom-pom hat wrestling with the heavy door of the barn before squeezing through the narrow gap.

The relief was both immediate and overwhelming, so much so that his fingers were trembling as he sent a quick text message to Brooke:

He's here.

Then he took a minute to allow his erratically beating heart to settle back inside his chest—and forward the brief message to Melissa—before he followed Brendan into the barn.

He caught up with him by the stall where Princess and her puppies had taken up residence. Although the gate was open, the boy remained outside, respecting the animals' space while mama nursed her babies.

"Hi, Mr. Patrick." Brendan greeted him as if there was nothing unusual about his presence at the ranch. "I came to see the puppies."

Patrick shoved his hands deep into the pockets of his jeans so that he wouldn't haul the boy into his arms and hug him tight, because he didn't want to freak Brendan out with such an unexpected display of emotion.

"Where's your mom?" he asked instead, wondering how Brooke's son would explain the current situation.

"She had to work late at the clinic."

"So how'd you get here?"

"I took the number three bus," Brendan told him.

Beneath the pride in his voice, there were hints of both defiance and worry. Yeah, the kid knew he was in trouble, but he had no idea how much.

"Does your mom know you're here?" Patrick asked.

The boy's gaze slid away, a telltale sign that he wasn't being entirely truthful when he said, "I told her I wanted to see the puppies."

"Did you tell your grandma, too?"

Now he shook his head.

"Do you think she might be worried, not knowing where you are?"

Brendan shrugged, but the way he hung his head confirmed that he was finally starting to realize the consequences of his actions.

Of course, neither of them could know the true extent of those consequences until Brooke arrived, and as Patrick directed the boy to the tack room to wait for his mom, he didn't envy her the worries and responsibilities of parenthood.

But maybe there was a tiny part of him that wished he could share them with her.

He's here.

The message on Brooke's screen blurred as the tears she'd been fighting to hold back finally broke through on a sob and spilled onto her cheeks.

"What is it?" her father asked, lifting one hand from the wheel to reach for hers.

She clutched it gratefully. "Brendan's at the Silver Star."

Bruce exhaled a breath. "That's a relief."

Her phone pinged with another message. "Mom's on her way, too. She found out from Russell that Brendan got on a different bus to go see the puppies." She swiped at the tears on her cheeks with the back of her free hand. "I'm so glad he's safe. And I'm so…"

"Furious," her dad suggested.

She nodded. "And hurt and disappointed and so many other emotions I can't even begin to decipher them all."

"The joys of parenting," Bruce remarked, squeezing her hand.

"How did you survive raising three kids?" she wondered aloud.

"I didn't do it on my own," her dad reminded her. "And you don't have to, either."

"Believe me, I know how lucky I am to have the support of you and Mom."

"Always," he said. "But I wasn't referring to us."

Did he mean…Patrick?

Did he know about her personal relationship with the rancher?

Of course he did, because she'd told her mom and her mom and dad had no secrets from one another.

But Brooke shoved those thoughts aside for now to focus on the only thing that really mattered: Brendan.

It seemed to take forever to get to the ranch, and Brooke had her seat belt unlatched before the vehicle was at a complete stop. She threw open the door and nearly tumbled to the ground, but Patrick was there. He caught her in his arms, and she was tempted, for just a moment, to lean into him and take strength from his strength.

Instead, she pulled away from him and squared her shoulders. "Where's Brendan?"

"He's in the tack room." Patrick stepped in front of her again, deliberately blocking her path.

"I need to see him," she said, hating that her voice hitched.

"I know." He set his hands on her shoulders, stroked them down her arms. "But I think it would be a good idea if we talked first about how you want to handle this, what you plan to say, so that I can back you up."

"I've barely had a chance to catch my breath, so I don't know what I'm going to say," she admitted, a hint of irritation in her tone. "But I know that I don't need you to back me up. This is between me and my son. It doesn't have anything to do with you."

Chapter Seventeen

Patrick dropped his hands from Brooke's arms and stepped back so that she could pass. She made an immediate beeline for the barn, swiping at the errant tears that spilled onto her cheeks along the way. He knew her emotions were running high and that he should probably cut her some slack, but he couldn't help feeling both hurt and frustrated by her determination to keep him on the periphery of her life.

"I guess that put me in my place."

"She didn't mean to lash out at you," Brooke's dad said, his tone gruff but sympathetic.

"Are you sure about that?" Patrick asked him.

"She was scared. We all were. When Brendan didn't get off the school bus, Sandra was frantic. And when she told me, I was frantic."

Patrick nodded his understanding, because he'd been frantic, too, when Brooke called to tell him.

"And I know it was a thousand times worse for Brooke," Bruce continued. "She's always tried so hard to be a good mom, and when something like this happens, a parent can't help but question every decision they've ever made.

"Add to that the fact that she has no one to share the responsibilities of parenting with, and she's carrying a hefty burden. Sure, she can take all the credit for raising a pretty terrific kid, but she also shoulders all the blame when something goes wrong."

"Good thing she has strong shoulders," Patrick remarked.

"They're strong because they've had to be. Because there haven't been many people in her life that she can count on."

Patrick got the message, loud and clear. If he wasn't ready to be the kind of man that Brooke—and Brendan—needed, then he had no business indulging in a romance with the single mom.

It was time for him to step up or step back.

Brooke tried to hold it together. She really did. But when she saw her little boy sitting on the edge of the bench in the tack room as if he'd been put in a time-out—and maybe he had—she couldn't hold it together anymore. And though Brendan likely didn't have a clue why his mother was crying as she hugged him so tight against her chest, he was soon crying, too.

"I'm sorry, Mommy," he said, when she'd finally managed to pull herself together again.

"I know," she said, still teary-eyed. "You're also grounded."

"What? Why?"

"Because this is one of those times when an apology doesn't make everything okay," she told him.

"But—"

"No buts," she interjected. "You know the rules, and you deliberately broke them."

"I didn't think not going to the Silver Star was a rule," Brendan protested.

"The rule is that you never go anywhere without asking permission and especially not without telling me where you're going," she reminded him.

"I didn't ask because I knew you'd say no," he admitted.

Brooke sighed, struggling to find the right words. "You might find this hard to believe, but I don't say no just for fun. When I tell you that you can't do something, there's usually a good reason. When I want to know where you are and who you're with at all times, it's because I need to know that you're safe."

"I *was* safe," he said. "I was *here*."

"But I didn't know that when Grandpa came to the clinic to tell me you didn't get off the bus," she pointed out. "And Gramma and Grandpa didn't know it, either. Which is why we've all been worried sick about you."

Fresh tears welled up in his eyes and he wrapped his arms around her, pressing his wet face against the front of her shirt. "I'm sorry," he said again.

And somehow the squeeze of his skinny arms managed to obliterate the last vestiges of terror that lingered in the corners of her heart.

And now that the fear had finally subsided, the questions pushed to the front of her mind, prompting her to ask, "How did you even get here?"

"I came on the number three bus."

Brooke frowned. "The bus drivers aren't supposed to let you get on any bus but your own," she said, uneasy to learn that he'd been able to walk onto the wrong vehicle.

He dropped his gaze to stare at his boots. "The usual bus driver wasn't driving today."

"But how did you even know what bus to take?"

"I asked Daniel Carson what was his bus."

Daniel was a grade ahead of Brendan at school, but they'd been in the same class when Daniel was in SK and Brendan was in JK. They'd had similar-looking backpacks that year and somehow mixed them up one day. Brendan had been inconsolable when he'd realized what happened, certain his mom wouldn't be able to pack his lunch for the next day if he didn't have his lunch box. So Brooke had driven out to Daniel's house to let the boys exchange bags.

Although that had been almost three years ago, she knew her son remembered the incident—and where Daniel lived, because he'd pointed out the house on various occasions when they'd driven past, wanting to know if she remembered "the boy who took my backpack."

"So you walked over here from Daniel's house?" she asked, still trying to put the pieces together—and not completely lose it again to realize that her son had crossed a major road between the two properties.

He nodded.

Even now, knowing he was safe, she felt sick to think of her seven-year-old child walking the rural road on his own. Because although he'd obviously reached his intended destination without mishap, there were so many things that could have gone wrong.

"I'm really glad that you're safe," Brooke said, aware that Patrick had returned to the barn and stood in the open doorway of the tack room, listening. "I'm also really mad that you disobeyed me after I said you couldn't come to the Silver Star today."

Brendan's lower lip trembled. "I just really wanted to see the puppies." Then he looked at Patrick, as if pleading for his help. "And you said I could come to the ranch anytime I wanted."

"With your mother's permission," the rancher reminded him. "What you did wasn't just against her rules, it was inconsiderate and potentially dangerous." He paused. "You also lied to *me*, Brendan, and that hurt my feelings. I thought we were friends. And friends should be honest with each other."

Patrick glanced at Brooke, then back at her son, and said regretfully, "So until you prove, to your mom's satisfaction—and mine, too—that you can follow her rules, you're not allowed at the Silver Star."

The boy's jaw dropped and his eyes filled with fresh tears before he spun on his heel and raced out of the room.

Brooke sighed and moved closer to the window,

through which she could watch Brendan run into the open arms of his grandmother, who'd obviously arrived while they were in the barn. Then Bruce folded his arms around both his wife and grandchild.

"You know, I always thought that whole 'punishing you hurts me more than it hurts you' thing parents tell their kids was a load of garbage," Patrick said. "But, damn, that was hard."

"Doing the right thing usually *is* hard," she agreed.

"How long is he grounded for?"

"I don't know yet. But thank you," she said. "For backing me up with Brendan."

"Always," he promised.

And in that moment, she caught a glimpse of what life might look like with a partner to share all the joys and sorrows, and she believed that Patrick Stafford just might be a man she could count on.

He didn't see Brooke at all over the next few days, and he thought that was probably a good thing. After the incident with Brendan and his conversation with the boy's grandfather, Patrick realized he had a lot of things he needed to figure out.

He'd told Bruce the truth when he said he couldn't imagine the roller-coaster emotions Brooke had gone through when her son was missing. Before he'd started spending time with Brooke and Brendan, Patrick hadn't appreciated the tremendous responsibilities that went hand in hand with raising a child—especially for a single parent.

Brooke deserved to be with someone who could take

some of that weight off her shoulders. A partner who was willing to share both the credit and the blame, the good times and bad times and scary-as-hell times. And as much as he might wish he could be that person, he knew that if he tried, he would only end up disappointing her.

The example that her parents had set in their relationship had given her something to aspire to, but he didn't know how to be a husband or a father. Certainly Derrick Stafford had never been a model of either. And while Patrick had learned a lot of what not to do, Brooke deserved better than that.

Now he was faced with the task of having to tell her the truth: that he was just one more guy she couldn't count on.

But he wasn't prepared to do it just yet, and he wasn't sure what to say when she drove up as he was cooling Pongo down after a ride.

Hopping out of her truck, she offered him a smile that squeezed his heart.

"I didn't expect to see you today," he said.

"I was passing by on my way back to town and thought I'd stop to invite you to dinner tomorrow night. It's my day off, which means that I'll actually have some time to cook," she said. "And hopefully figure out how to apologize for the way I reacted the other day when Brendan was missing. Or after he was found."

"Please don't apologize," he said, aware that he was going to do something worse than bruise her feelings and with less justification.

"So…dinner?" she prompted.

"Actually, Melissa's trying out a new chicken-fried steak and gravy recipe tomorrow."

"Oh. Okay." She looked at him then, as if waiting for him to say something more.

He remained silent.

"This would be a good time for you to invite me to have dinner with you here instead," she said, with a hopeful smile.

He was more than a little tempted to do just that, and to put off what needed to be done. But that wouldn't be fair to either of them.

"You grounded Brendan," he reminded her.

"I'm sure my parents would be happy to have Brendan stay with them. And since I'm not grounded, I could even stay for dessert," she said.

It was obvious what she was offering, and it seemed like forever since they'd made love…

But since when did he think of sex as making love?

And since when did he think about a woman every minute of every day that they were apart?

Only since Brooke.

She was always on his mind and in his heart.

The terrifying truth was that she meant more to him than any woman he'd dated in a very long time, maybe ever. And he could easily imagine a life with her and Brendan, but he wasn't ready to be a husband and father, to be tied down with a family.

"Actually, I don't think that's a good idea," he said.

The teasing smile on her face faded, and the light in her eyes dimmed. "Why not?"

He could tell by the flatness of her tone that she

already knew what he was going to say. But she was going to make him say it. She was going to make him prove he was every bit the callous jerk he'd promised her he wouldn't be.

"I just think…it's been a crazy week with everyone's emotions running high and maybe— I think maybe it's time to take a step back."

"A step back." She nodded. "I guess that puts us right back where we started, doesn't it?"

"I'm sorry, Brooke."

"No, I'm the one who's sorry," she said. "Sorry that I let myself believe you might be different. That I believed *you* when you said you cared about me and Brendan, that we mattered."

"I *do* care about you and Brendan," he told her. "I'm just not ready to take on the responsibilities of a wife and child."

"Whoa!" She held up both hands. "I invited you to dinner. I didn't ask you to marry me."

"But isn't that where you thought our relationship was eventually headed?" he challenged.

"Eventually is a rather vague timeline," she pointed out. "And even if it did cross my mind that we might *eventually* move in that direction, I can assure you that I'm in no rush to tie myself to a cowboy with a reputation for bailing at the first sign of a relationship getting real."

"That's not what's happening here," he protested, though the denial sounded hollow even to his own ears.

"That's exactly what's happening," she said. "And truthfully, I'm not surprised. Maybe this relationship charade lasted a little longer than I expected, but we both knew this was where we'd end up, didn't we?"

And without giving him a chance to respond, she got back in her truck and drove away.

Brooke had told him that she wasn't surprised, but she was.

Not only surprised but hurt.

Just when she'd started to think that she'd been wrong about him, that there was more to Patrick Stafford than his reputation, he'd proved her not just a fool but a lousy judge of character.

Thankfully, she didn't have to come up with any excuses to justify to Brendan why they weren't going out to the Silver Star, because he was grounded. And maybe by the time his grounding was lifted, he would have forgotten about Patrick and the Silver Star.

But as angry as she was with Patrick, she couldn't deny that there had been some truth to his accusation. She'd agreed to an affair, and then she'd started to imagine the physical intimacy might lead to something more. Because she wanted more, not just for herself, but for her son, too.

She wanted a man who wanted to be a father to Brendan, but now she knew Patrick wasn't ever going to be that man. And if she'd been hurt by the realization, it was her own fault. Because he'd told her right from the beginning that he wasn't looking to take on that kind of responsibility.

Of course, he'd then spent a couple of months doing a pretty good imitation of a man taking on that responsibility. But that was all it had been—an imitation. She deserved the real thing. And so did Brendan.

Jenna and Melissa were in the kitchen, eating caramel apple coffee cake and drinking herbal tea, when Patrick walked into the house. He usually couldn't wait to sample whatever his cousin had whipped up, but he wasn't the least bit tempted by the freshly baked treat today, his belly filled with a hard, heavy ball of guilt and regrets.

Jenna glanced past him, as if looking for someone else. "I thought I saw Brooke's truck in the driveway."

"Yeah, she was here," he confirmed.

"She usually pops in to say hi," Melissa remarked.

"She had to get home."

Though he'd attempted to keep his tone neutral, the look exchanged by the two women warned that he hadn't quite succeeded.

"Oh, Patrick. What did you do?" Jenna asked him.

"What do you mean?" he hedged.

"You broke up with her, didn't you?" His sister's tone was accusing.

"How do you break up with someone you aren't really dating?" he challenged, unnerved by the eerily accurate insights of the women.

"He didn't break up with her," Melissa said, speaking to Jenna now. "He did something worse—he broke her heart."

"I did not," he denied.

His sister folded her arms over her chest. "Did you make her cry?"

"No."

"She wouldn't cry in front of him," Melissa decided. "She's stronger than that."

"Or maybe because she agreed that it was time to go our separate ways," he offered.

"I don't understand," Jenna said, sounding sincerely baffled and maybe a little disappointed. "I thought she was different. I thought you really cared about her."

"I did. I do," he admitted. "But the longer we let things continue, the more everyone was going to be hurt when it was over."

"Why did it ever have to be over?" his sister demanded. "Why couldn't you, for once, let yourself actually be happy?"

"I am happy," he said. "I like my life the way it is. I'm not looking for a ready-made family and I definitely don't need the complication or the responsibility of a child."

Jenna shook her head. "You really don't see it, do you?"

"See what?"

"You only *think* you don't want a family, because you don't want a family like the screwed-up one we grew up in—and no one can blame you for that," she said. "But while you've been renovating buildings and fixing fences over the past several months, you've also been creating a family here."

"Is there alcohol in that cake?" he asked Melissa, suggesting that might be the cause of his sister's nonsensical rambling.

"Pregnant," she reminded him. "And your sister isn't just sober, she's insightful, and you should listen to her."

"You might not realize you're doing it, but you instinctively care for and nurture everyone under your roof," Jenna continued. "Melissa, me and even Princess."

"I'm letting you stay—*temporarily*—in an empty room, and Melissa works here," he pointed out.

The women exchanged another glance.

"Denial," they said in unison.

He just shook his head.

"Whether you want one or not, you've got a family right here," Jenna continued. "But until you fix things with Brooke, it's going to be incomplete."

Of course, it took Patrick a few days to come around to the realization that his sister was right.

For a guy who claimed to not want complications, his life was full of them: he had a dog and six puppies in his barn, a runaway sister in his guest cottage and a pregnant woman in his attic.

But what he didn't have—and the only things he really wanted—were Brooke and Brendan.

He picked up the phone to invite her to come out to the Silver Star, then put it down again, suspecting his request would be refused. He considered calling the clinic to ask her to come out to the ranch to check on his animals, but knew she'd see right through that ruse and probably send the other Dr. B. Langley in her stead. Which left him with only one option: to grovel on her turf.

Maybe it had taken him a while to come around

to the realization that they were meant to be together, but he had to hope that he wasn't too late to convince Brooke to give him—to give them—a second chance.

Brooke saw the appointment on her schedule when she arrived at the clinic Wednesday morning.

2:00 Patrick Stafford—puppy exams/shots

She'd known it was inevitable that their paths would eventually cross—after all, her father wouldn't always be available to take every appointment she wanted to avoid—but she'd expected to have more time to put the broken pieces of her heart back together first.

But two o'clock was manageable, she decided. Maybe a few hours wouldn't be enough time to fix her heart, but it would be enough to put up her shields and a professional smile on her face.

"Good afternoon, Mr. Stafford," she said, greeting him as she would any other pet owner—polite and professional.

"Hello, Brooke."

She didn't respond to his familiar address, but her cool reserve began to melt when he opened the door of the crate and the puppies tumbled out onto the floor, climbing over one another in their excitement to escape the confined space.

"Oh…they've gotten so big," she said, automatically crouching to give them the adoration they craved. Because while she might want to hold herself aloof from the rancher, she was helpless to resist these babies.

"They're six weeks old now," he said, as if she might have forgotten that she'd not only been there but played a key role in bringing them into the world.

"Time for their first shots," she confirmed. She scooped up the nearest puppy, her fingers sinking into the soft fur as she lifted it to read the name on its tag. "Hello, Han."

The pup answered by swiping his tiny tongue over her chin, making her smile even as her heart was breaking all over again.

"I also want to be sure they're in good health before I let them go to their adoptive families," Patrick said.

"Have you found homes for all of them?" She gently lowered the puppy to the scale to check his weight.

"All except Leia."

"No one wanted her?" she asked, surprised.

"There was interest," he said. "But I thought about what Brendan said and decided to let her stay with her mom."

"So you'll have Princess and Leia," she realized.

He nodded.

She refused to believe it meant anything that he'd chosen to keep the puppy her son had wanted as his own.

"And my grandfather's taking Luke, and Sarah has claimed Han, so the original trilogy are all going to be close to home."

"That's nice," she said, as she continued to examine the puppies—taking temperatures, listening to their hearts, checking their eyes and ears.

"Finn looks like he might find a permanent home

next door, Rey was claimed by my cousin Ashley, and your vet tech has dibs on Rose."

"Courtney's been talking about getting a puppy for almost a year," Brooke noted. "Being the first one to hold Rose after she was born must have convinced her it was time."

"Are you sure you haven't changed your mind about wanting one?" he asked.

"I've changed my mind at least a hundred times," she admitted. "But my reasons for not taking one haven't.

"There you go," she said, setting the last pup back in the crate he'd used to transport them to the clinic.

"Thanks." He latched the door.

"You can settle up with Larissa at reception," she said, prodding him to move along.

"I will," he promised, but still made no move to leave.

"Was there something else you wanted?" she finally asked.

"Yeah, I want you to come over for dinner this weekend. You and Brendan," he hastened to clarify. "Assuming he's over being grounded by then."

"Why?" she asked, not just surprised by the invitation but a little wary, too.

"Because I've missed you," he confessed. "Both of you."

She wasn't going to let herself be swayed by the sincerity in his voice. And she certainly wasn't going to set her son—or herself—up for more disappointment.

"I screwed up in a big way, and I just want a chance to explain…and maybe to make it up to you. What do you say?" he cajoled. "Friday or Saturday—your choice."

She wanted to rant and scream in frustration that he couldn't shove them away one minute and expect them to come back the next. But she didn't want him to know how much his rejection had hurt her, so she only shook her head and said, "I'm going to be out of town this weekend."

"Where are you going?"

"A veterinarian conference in San Diego."

"This is the conference you mentioned a few weeks back—the one you weren't sure would be worth your time?" he guessed.

She nodded. It was also the one she'd considered inviting him to attend with her, so she wouldn't have to sleep alone. But of course she wasn't going to mention that now.

"Why'd you change your mind about going?" he asked.

"I found out that a friend from college is presenting the findings from a new study on bovine respiratory syncytial virus," she said.

"I have to wonder if you really want to learn more about BRSV or if you just want to put some distance between us."

"I think you've already done that," she pointed out.

"I was an idiot," he said.

But she shook her head. "No, you were right. Things were getting too intense. Too real."

"I want it to be real," he told her. "I want you, me and Brendan to be together. A family."

It was everything she'd dreamed of—and everything he'd said he didn't want. "Where is this coming from all of a sudden?"

"It's not all of a sudden," he denied. "I know it probably seems like it is, but that's only because I refused to recognize what was in my heart."

"Barely a week ago, you told me that you wanted to take a step back," she reminded him.

"A week ago, I was scared and stupid. Now I'm just scared, because what I feel for you and for Brendan is strong and real, and it terrifies me to imagine my life without both of you in it.

"And I'm screwing this up again," he realized. "Because I skipped over the most important part. That I love you, Brooke."

"No," she said, looking away so he wouldn't see the tears that filled her eyes. So he wouldn't guess the desperate longing in her heart that wanted to propel her into his arms. "You can't do this. You can't come in here and tell me that you love me and expect it to make everything okay."

"Then tell me what I can do," he urged. "Tell me what you want."

"I want you to go so Larissa can bring the next patient into this room."

Chapter Eighteen

"Melissa—hi. Come on in."

"I apologize for stopping by unannounced," Patrick's cousin said. "But I made peanut butter cookies today, and I wanted to drop some off for you before they all disappeared."

"That was really thoughtful," Brooke said. "And now that I've got cookies, I think a cup of tea is in order. Care to join me?"

"A cup of tea sounds wonderful," Melissa agreed.

Brooke led her into the apartment and turned on the kettle. "What kind do you like?"

"Do you have anything without caffeine?"

"Peppermint, lemon and decaffeinated Earl Grey," she offered.

"Hmm...the Earl Grey sounds good," Melissa decided.

Brooke made the tea, then opened the container of cookies and set half a dozen on a plate in the middle of the table.

"So how are you doing?" Melissa asked, when Brooke sat down across from her.

"I'm okay," she said. It wasn't exactly the truth—between the drama of Brendan's bus adventure, being dumped by Patrick and then his visit to the clinic, she felt as if she'd been strapped into an emotional roller coaster—but she thought she was doing a pretty good job of faking it.

"I can't imagine anything more terrifying for a parent than not knowing where her child is," the other woman confided.

"It's definitely not an experience I ever want to repeat," Brooke told her.

"So how long is Brendan grounded for?"

"I'm still trying to figure that out. My gut instinct was to say until he's sixteen, but even in the heat of the moment I realized that was a little extreme."

"But understandable," Melissa said.

Brooke smiled, grateful for the expectant mom's support. "But now I think my memories of the terror might subside enough that I'll be willing to let him out of my sight in about six months."

"Does that mean you're taking him to San Diego with you?"

"Obviously Patrick told you about my trip?"

Melissa nodded.

"I wish I could take Brendan with me, but he'd be bored to tears—or he'd convince his aunt Lori to take him to Disneyland, which would hardly fit the definition of a grounding," she said, with a shake of her head. "So he'll stay here with my parents."

"I met your mom and dad at the ranch that day," Melissa said. "They were amazing—so calm and cool despite everything going on."

"They are great," she acknowledged. "I definitely lucked out there."

"Patrick wasn't nearly as lucky."

"And now we get to the real reason for your visit?" Brooke guessed.

"I really did come to see you—and to bring you cookies. But maybe I also wanted to plead my cousin's case a little," Melissa admitted.

"There's no case and, therefore, no pleading required. He's the one who decided that everything was getting a little too real."

"If you knew about his relationship with his parents, you'd understand why Patrick tries not to get too attached," his cousin told her.

"I know they split up a few times but always got back together," Brooke said.

"It might have been better for their kids if they didn't always get back together," Melissa confided. "My family moved to Seattle when I was ten, but before then, I spent a lot of time with my cousins. And in the years that followed, I'd often come to Haven for a week in the summer and Sarah and Jenna would come to Seattle for a week after Christmas, or vice versa."

"It's nice that you were able to stay close," Brooke said.

"It was," the other woman agreed. "But one time when I was there, Uncle Derrick and Aunt Liz got into a big fight. I don't remember what it was about, or if I even knew what it was about, because it seemed that an argument about one thing inevitably turned into something else.

"Anyway, later that night, when I thought the fighting was over, I went down to the kitchen to get a drink and I heard Uncle Derrick grumbling about something 'his son' had done, and Aunt Liz shot back saying 'maybe he's not your son.'"

Brooke sucked in a breath.

"That was my reaction, too," Melissa said. "And not wanting to hear any more of what they were saying, I turned around to tiptoe back up the stairs—and almost ran right into Patrick."

"He heard?"

Melissa nodded. "A few months later, Derrick and Liz split up. When Jenna and Sarah came to Washington over the Christmas break, they told me that their dad had demanded a paternity test."

Now Brooke winced.

"No one believed Liz had ever cheated on her husband—except maybe Derrick, and probably only to ease his guilty conscience. But even if there was a possibility Patrick wasn't Derrick's biological child, he'd raised him since birth, so you'd think DNA wouldn't matter as much as the bond they shared."

And Brooke didn't doubt that his father's willingness to disregard that bond would have struck a harsh blow to their relationship.

"His parents each used him as a weapon in their efforts to hurt one another, never considering that their son would be the one to carry the deepest scars."

"I had no idea," Brooke said. "I mean, I know he isn't particularly close to either of his parents..."

"And now you know why."

And knowing, she couldn't help but hurt for the rejected boy, but that didn't mean she was willing to forgive the man who'd rejected her and her son.

"I think Patrick didn't want to get involved with you because he worried that he wouldn't be able to love a child who wasn't his. Because that's the message he got from his father's demand for a paternity test. But then when Brendan was missing, he panicked because he realized that he already did love him, and the prospect of losing him was more than he could bear."

"Instead, he pushed him—pushed both of us— away," Brooke pointed out.

"And immediately regretted it," Melissa said.

She sighed. "So what am I supposed to do now?"

"What do you want to do?"

"I don't know," Brooke confided. "I was so hurt when he walked away, even if it only proved that he was exactly the type of guy he always claimed to be. But then he came into the clinic and asked for another chance, and now... I don't know what I'm supposed to feel."

"There is no 'supposed to' about feelings," the other woman said wisely. "So I'd suggest you stop trying to reason this out in your head and listen to your heart."

"But how many chances am I supposed to give him?" she asked. "How many times am I supposed to put my heart—and my son's—on the line?"

"I'm hardly an expert, but I'd say that depends."

"On what?" Brooke wondered.

"Whether or not you're in love with him."

He'd screwed up.

If he'd had any doubts that he was 100 percent at fault, both of Patrick's sisters and his cousin were only too happy to reassure him on that point. And to offer all kinds of unsolicited advice. But while he appreciated their interest and concern, he decided that what he really needed was a junior consultant.

He knew he was taking a big risk. Brooke had been clear from the beginning that she didn't want Brendan to know about his mom's relationship with "Mr. Patrick." She didn't want to raise her son's hopes that a few dates might lead to something more.

And he'd gone along, because he figured she knew her kid a lot better than he did—which of course she did. But as a result of this effort to manage Brendan's expectations, she'd succeeded in keeping her own little world intact—and Patrick on the outside looking in.

He didn't want to be on the outside anymore.

So, yeah, he was about to take a big risk, but he was looking for a big reward.

And Saturday afternoon, after Brendan's grounding had been lifted and he was allowed to visit the ranch, the boy played with Princess and her puppies until they were all played out and ready for a nap. Patrick then invited him into the house for milk and cookies and what he hoped he might someday look back on as his first father-son chat with the boy.

Not entirely sure where to begin, he said, "Do you remember when we talked before about your mom not having a boyfriend?"

Brendan, his mouth full of cookie, nodded.

Patrick tucked his sweaty palms into the front pockets of his jeans. "Well, I was thinking about what you said…and I've decided I'd like to ask her to be my girlfriend. If it's still okay with you."

"It's more than okay," the boy said. "It's awesome!"

"I'm glad you think so," he said, aware that he was manipulating the situation—and possibly Brooke's son—to get the boy on his side. But considering how spectacularly Patrick had struck out on his own, he knew it was time to bring in new talent. "But I think it might take some work to convince your mom."

"You could try giving her flowers," Brendan suggested.

It was solid advice, he acknowledged, and a little embarrassing to realize the kid had pointed out a basic courtship ritual he'd completely overlooked.

"Girls get all mushy when you give them flowers," the boy added sagely.

"How many girls have you given flowers to?" Patrick asked him.

Brendan rolled his eyes at the question. "None, but Grandpa gives them to Gramma all the time, and even if she's mad at him, she stops being mad and they kiss."

"Flowers are a good idea," Patrick agreed, smothering a laugh. "Kissing is even better."

Brendan made a face.

"Don't knock it until you try it," he said, then hastily revised his advice. "But don't be in any rush to try it."

"I've tried it," the boy told him. "Ruby asked me to push her on the swings at school, and 'cause I did, she kissed me and said I was her boyfriend."

"Where did she kiss you?" he wondered.

"By the swings," Brendan said again.

"I mean— Never mind," he said, deciding he wasn't ready to tackle the various issues involved with girls and dating, but also making a mental note to keep Ruby away from the boy he hoped would soon be his son. "Back to the flowers. Do you know if there's any particular kind of flowers your mom would like?"

"Yellow ones."

Patrick nodded. "Okay, then, let's go do some shopping."

When Brooke FaceTimed with Brendan Saturday night from her hotel room, her son was full of excitement as a result of his visit to the Silver Star—his first return to the ranch since his grounding was lifted.

The previous night, when Sandra told her Patrick had invited Brendan to visit, Brooke had considered not letting him go. But she knew it wasn't fair to punish her son again because she was hurting, so she gave permission but left it up to her mom to decide if she wanted to take him. Of course, Sandra had never been able to refuse her grandson anything.

And as Brendan regaled her with puppy tales, Brooke could tell he was overjoyed to learn that Patrick had decided to keep Leia, and also sad to know that most of the other puppies would soon be going to different homes.

"But at least I'll get to see Princess and Leia whenever we visit the Silver Star," he said.

Damn, maybe she should have let him have a puppy. If she had, he'd be less likely to notice when he didn't get invited back to the ranch that had almost become a second home to him over the past couple of months. But right now, she didn't have the heart to tell him that there were unlikely to be many visits to the ranch in their future.

"And you might find Rose at the clinic sometimes," she said instead. "Because her new home is going to be with Courtney."

"Yay!" he said.

They chatted for a few more minutes, and though Brooke purposely didn't ask her son about Patrick, that didn't stop her from thinking about him. And wondering if he'd really meant it when he said he wanted a second chance.

If it was possible that he really did love her.

She'd hoped that getting out of town—and away from Patrick—for a few days might help her clear her head and sort out her emotions so that she could start to get over him. But after his visit to the clinic earlier in the week, a tiny blossom of hope had begun to unfurl inside her heart. Hope that she wouldn't have to get over him but might instead be able to look toward a future for them together.

You, me and Brendan... A family.

She pushed the enticing thought to the back of her mind and made her way to the restaurant where she was meeting Lori and Matt for dinner.

But the whole time she was seated across the table from her friend and her new beau, Brooke couldn't forget the question Melissa had asked. She'd pretended she didn't know the answer, because she didn't want to be in love with Patrick. Because being in love required openness and vulnerability, which, experience had taught her, could result in hurt.

Except that being with the happy couple also reminded Brooke that love could result in healing. Lori and Matt had each been in relationships with other people before, but those unsuccessful experiences hadn't held them back from taking another chance and finding a true connection together.

By the time she went back to her empty hotel room alone, she'd made a decision. Not about whether or not she was in love with Patrick, because that had never really been in question, but to finally tell him the truth about her feelings.

It was almost dinnertime when Brooke finally arrived home from San Diego on Sunday. She'd texted her mom with her ETA when her plane landed, only to learn that her parents were going out to eat and wouldn't be there when she arrived. After two and a half days away, she was disappointed to have to wait even longer still to see Brendan and give him the bag of saltwater taffy she'd brought back from Ocean Beach.

Preoccupied by these thoughts, it took her a moment to realize that the lights were on inside her apartment when she opened the door, and another to register the scent of…toast?

"Hello?" she said cautiously.

"It's Mom!"

Brendan raced out of the kitchen and threw his arms around her. Patrick followed at a more measured pace and paused a few feet away, as if uncertain of his reception. That made two of them.

"Welcome home," he said.

"I…didn't expect anyone to be here," she said.

"We wanted to surprise you," Brendan said, squeezing tight.

She hugged him back, happy to see him…and not quite sure what to read into Patrick's presence, though her hopeful heart was leaning in a very specific direction.

Stop trying to reason this out in your head and listen to your heart.

"Are you surprised?" Brendan asked now.

"Very," she confirmed, realizing that her mother had obviously been in on whatever this plan was.

"Are you happy surprised or mad surprised?" Patrick asked cautiously. "Because if you're mad, I take full responsibility."

"I'm…still-evaluating surprised," she said.

"We got you flowers," Brendan said, drawing her attention to the beautiful arrangement of yellow roses, gerberas and tulips set in the middle of the table. "Do you like them?"

"Oh." She felt a flutter in her belly. "Yes, I do. They're beautiful."

Her gaze shifted back to Patrick, who was watching her with such focus and intensity, she felt that flutter again.

"Brendan, why don't you take your mom's bag to her room?" he suggested.

"Okay," her son agreed, pulling out the handle and wheeling it away.

"If you wanted to get him out of the room, you just bought yourself about twelve seconds because my bedroom isn't very far."

"I remember where your bedroom is. And, yes, I thought you'd probably want him out of the room when I did this," he said, sliding his arms around her.

Though she thought they should talk before they moved on to other things, she didn't balk at being drawn closer. And when he lowered his mouth to kiss her, she couldn't help but respond—her lips softening, her body melting.

Conscious of the twelve seconds she'd allotted, he reluctantly eased his mouth from hers. "Welcome home."

"You said that already," she told him.

"Did I tell you that I missed you?"

She shook her head. "No."

"Well, I did. And not just this weekend, but every day of the week before that, when I was foolish enough to think I could ever live without you."

"I missed you, too, but—"

"Are you hungry?" he asked.

She wasn't sure if he'd cut her off because Brendan had returned to the room or if he didn't want to hear how she might finish that thought.

Either way, there was only one answer to his question. "Starved."

"Good, because dinner is ready."

"I thought something smelled good when I walked in."

"And I thought it was you that smelled good enough to eat," he said, lowering his head to nibble her throat.

She took a step back, her cheeks flushing with heat as Brendan giggled.

It made her happy to hear her son happy, and while Brendan had never been a shy child, he'd positively blossomed under Patrick's attention. But why should she be surprised that her little boy had fallen in love with the rancher when she'd done the same thing?

Yes, she'd been hurt and angry when he'd brushed her off, but the residue of those feelings couldn't dim the brightness of the love that filled her heart.

And maybe it was scary to think about giving him another chance, but it was a lot scarier to think about living the rest of her life without the man she loved.

So they sat on their knees at the coffee table and ate to-die-for grilled cheese—which Brendan helped make—followed by Sweet Caroline's Twelve-Layer Chocolate Bliss for dessert.

When Brendan had licked the last remnants of icing off his fork, he leaned over and stage-whispered to Patrick, "When are you gonna ask her?"

"Apparently right now," Patrick said.

"Well, *do* it," her son urged.

Brooke watched the interaction between them—one a little impatient, the other a little bit nervous.

"Ask me what?" she asked warily, thinking her son might have somehow finagled the promise of a puppy from the rancher.

"If you'll be my girlfriend, and maybe go out on a date with me sometime," Patrick replied.

Not a puppy, but something much bigger, she realized.

And she understood the significance of him making the request in front of her son. He wasn't just asking her to go out for dinner or to a movie, but to acknowledge that they were in a relationship together. He was asking her to take a chance—to give their relationship a chance.

Don't you think it's time...to take a chance and finally let yourself be happy?

"I will," she agreed.

"Yay!" Brendan cheered and pumped his chocolate-smeared fist in the air, prompting Brooke to send her son to wash up and get ready for bed.

When Patrick gathered the dessert plates to take them to the kitchen, she followed to help tidy up. But he had other ideas.

Better ideas, she decided, when he kissed her, long and slow and deep.

And then he said, "I love you, Brooke. I know those words don't make everything okay but—"

She touched her fingers to his lips to halt the flow of words and replied simply, "I love you, too."

When the kitchen was tidied, Patrick and Brooke returned to the living room. Brendan, having brushed his teeth and changed into his pj's, snuggled up on the sofa with them.

Together. A family.

"I've been thinking about something," Brendan suddenly announced.

And Patrick had a sneaking suspicion he knew what that "something" was.

"What have you been thinking about?" Brooke asked her son.

"I don't wanna be the third Dr. Langley."

"That's okay." Brooke ruffled his hair affectionately. "You've got lots of time to figure out what you want to do with your life."

"I wanna be a vet," he said. "But I wanna be the *second* Dr. Stafford."

"You can't just change your name, Brendan."

"I can change mine if you change yours," he said.

Patrick sighed. "You really don't understand what 'later' means, do you?" he said to Brendan.

"I'm impatient," the boy reminded him.

"I know," he admitted.

Brooke looked at Patrick then, a slight furrow between her brows. "I think I'm missing something here."

"That's because your son skipped a few steps ahead. What Brendan was supposed to say—but not until you'd had some time to get used to dating me," he said, with a pointed look at the child, "is that you could be the first Dr. Stafford…if you agreed to marry me."

Then he pulled the ring box out of his pocket and opened it to reveal a three-and-a-half-carat diamond solitaire set in a platinum band.

"Ohmygod." The words were a whispered prayer as hope bloomed inside her more abundantly than the flowers on the table.

"Do you like it? I picked it out," her son said proudly. "It's a princess cut." He looked up at Patrick. "Did I get that right?"

She had to laugh. "Of course it's a princess cut. And of course I like it, but…" She looked helplessly at Patrick, stunned and overwhelmed. "Don't you think this is happening a little fast?"

He shook his head. "I think I've been waiting for you my whole life."

"But are you sure you're ready to get married?" she asked. "It's a pretty big step from girlfriend to fiancée in one night."

"And I can't wait for you to be my wife, so that you and Brendan can come to live with me at the Silver Star."

"And I want to live at the Silver Star and finally have a dad," Brendan chimed in.

"So what do you say, Brooke? Will you marry me so that we can all live together and Brendan can call me 'Dad' instead of 'Mr. Patrick'?"

"Say 'yes,' Mom."

"You better be sure about this," she warned Patrick. "Because if I say 'yes,' it's forever."

"Well, that's good," he said, holding her gaze so that

she could see the truth and depth of his feelings in his eyes. "Because I want you—both of you—forever."

"In that case, my answer is yes," she told him.

"Yay!" Brendan cheered.

Brooke suspected he'd also pumped his fist in the air, but she didn't see it because Patrick was kissing her.

"I told you she'd kiss you if you gave her flowers," the boy said smugly.

"You did indeed," Patrick agreed.

"And how is it that my son is an expert on kissing and flowers?" Brooke wondered.

"It's a long story that starts with his grandparents and leads to a girl named Ruby."

She decided the story could wait till another time.

After all, they were going to have a lifetime together.

* * * * *

*Look for Skylar Gilmore's story,
the next book in
award-winning author Brenda Harlen's
Match Made in Haven miniseries,
coming in August 2020, wherever
Harlequin Special Edition books
and ebooks are sold.*

1218

Love Harlequin romance?

DISCOVER.

Be the first to find out about promotions,
news and exclusive content!

 Facebook.com/HarlequinBooks

Twitter.com/HarlequinBooks

 Instagram.com/HarlequinBooks

Pinterest.com/HarlequinBooks

ReaderService.com

EXPLORE.

Sign up for the Harlequin e-newsletter and
download a free book from any series at
TryHarlequin.com

CONNECT.

Join our Harlequin community to
share your thoughts and connect
with other romance readers!
Facebook.com/groups/HarlequinConnection